Antiques Wanted

Antiques Wanted

A Trash 'n' Treasures Mystery

Barbara Allan

KENSINGTON BOOKS
http://www.kensingtonbooks.com

KENSINGTON BOOKS are published by

Kensington Publishing Corp.
119 West 40th Street
New York, NY 10018

Copyright © 2018 by Max Allan Collins and Barbara Collins

All Kensington titles, imprints, and distributed lines are available at special quantity discounts for bulk purchases for sales promotion, premiums, fund-raising, educational, or institutional use. Special book excerpts or customized printings can also be created to fit specific needs. For details, write or phone the office of the Kensington Special Sales Manager: Attn. Special Sales Department. Kensington Publishing Corp., 119 West 40th Street, New York, NY 10018. Phone: 1-800-221-2647.

Kensington and the K logo Reg. U.S. Pat. & TM Off.

Library of Congress Card Catalogue Number: 2017955131

ISBN-13: 978-1-4967-1137-3
ISBN-10: 1-4967-1137-8
First Kensington Hardcover Edition: May 2018

eISBN-13: 978-1-4967-1139-7
eISBN-10: 1-4967-1139-4
First Kensington Electronic Edition: May 2018

10 9 8 7 6 5 4 3 2 1

Printed in the United States of America

For Carol Gorman,
knowing Ed would smile

Brandy's Quote:
Mothers are all slightly insane.
—J. D. Salinger

Mother's Quote:
Nothing's so sacred as honor
and nothing's so loyal as love.
—Wyatt Earp

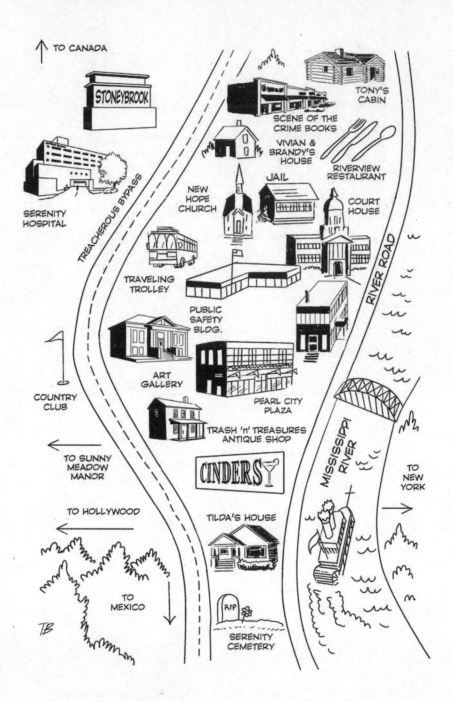

Chapter One

Support Your Loco Sheriff

Where to begin? Well, how about with the fact that Mother is running for county sheriff?

What!?! (you might well ask). *Is that even possible? I thought the position was appointed by the mayor with the approval of the city council.*

So did I! But voters have always picked the sheriff. And now that the current sheriff, Peter J. Rudder, is stepping down due to health concerns, there's going to be a special election in a couple of months—and you know how many friends Mother has.

Didn't you try to stop her?

What do you think? I told her that she had no experience, no aptitude, no qualifications whatsoever.

And what did she say?

She said, "Dear, lots of people hold office who aren't qualified."

Who could refute that? But surely there are some *qualifications.*

Surprisingly little! For our county, the candidate must be at least twenty-five years old, been a resident here for no less than one year, and have a minimum of 160 hours of law enforcement training at an accredited law enforcement school—which Mother got several years ago taking night classes at the community college, after solving her first murder case.

Oh, brother . . . Maybe you should contact her psychiatrist for his help.

I did.

And?

He refused to talk to me on grounds of patient confidentiality. And *my* therapist's advice to me, before you ask, was to stay on my antidepressant.

Wow. Maybe you should just get out of town. You know, on the next stage.

That's your solution? Leave town? And I'll handle the sarcasm, thank you very much.

Leaving out the back door is what I'd *do if she were* my *mother.*

Not helpful!

Hey, you came to me. You seemed to want my opinion, and I gave it.

Sorry, you're right—I'm just a little stressed.

Look, the voters aren't stupid—they care about who's serving and protecting them. So you can be outwardly supportive while inwardly secure in the fact that she'll never win.

You think?

Sure . . . but keep a suitcase packed and ready.

The *she* in *she'll never win* (for you newcomers) is Vivian Borne, midseventies, Danish stock, attractive despite large, out-of-fashion glasses that magnify her eyes, widowed, bipolar, legendary local thespian, and even more legendary amateur sleuth.

She-Who-Is-a-Little-Stressed is me, Brandy Borne, thirty-three, divorced, blond by choice, Prozac-popping prodigal daughter who came home from Chicago, postdivorce, to live with her mother in the small Mississippi River town of Serenity, Iowa, seeking solitude and relaxation but instead finding herself the frequent reluctant accomplice in Vivian Borne's escapades. Did I mention reluctant?

The third member of our household (and possibly the smartest) is Sushi, my diabetic shih tzu who once was blind but now can see, which sounds oddly spiritual for a dog, but really just means she had successful cataract surgery.

On what appeared to be just another Monday morning, Trash 'n' Treasures—the antiques shop Mother and I run together—was closed for the day. That left us pajama-clad, lingering leisurely over breakfast at the Duncan Phyfe table in the dining room.

Because the meal Mother had made was better than our usual fare—egg casserole, homemade hash, crisp bacon, sausage patties, and giant frosted cinnamon rolls—I suspected the elder Borne had something more in store for me that was not so palatable.

Finally, unable to munch down another morsel, I sat back and sighed, being far too ladylike to burp (as far as you know).

"Well," I said, "let's have the check."

Mother, seated opposite, gazed at me with a dewy-eyed innocence right out of a silent movie. "The check, dear?"

I gestured to the dishes around us. "All that couldn't have been free. Has there been a murder? Do you need me to stage-manage your next one-woman show? Let's get it over with."

Mother lay a splayed hand to her chest. "My darling girl, your mistrust and suspicions cut me deep."

Darling girl? This was going to be a rough one. A grunt of a response was all I could manage (sort of a half grunt, half burp). (Okay, so I'm not so ladylike.)

"Still," she went on, at once casual and grand, "I do

have something in mind for today. Shall we retire to the library?"

Bedlam would have been more like it, but the library was—in addition to being a music and TV den—Mother's incident room when she and I (did I mention reluctant?) were on a case.

Mother stood from the table and smoothed the front of her 1940s pink chenille robe with shoulder pads, apparently on loan from Joan Crawford, an item of apparel she'd refused to give up even after I'd bought her a nice new robe for Christmas. (Once, I tried throwing the ratty old thing out with the trash, but she managed to retrieve it before the garbage truck came by. For someone with glasses that thick, she has sharp eyes.)

I followed Mother into the library/music/TV/incident room, which was redolent of ancient moldy books, smelly old brass instruments (mostly cornets), and air freshener—a lethal combination to inhale on a full stomach.

She gestured for me to sit on the bench of an antiquated stand-up piano that neither of us could play. Oh. Reminds me. For about a month there was another smell added to the room's fragrant bouquet: a dead mouse, which had gotten strangled in the piano wires. Accident, suicide, or murder—that one we never solved.

(**Note to Brandy from Editor:** *While I understand you are going through a difficult time with Vivian, readers come to these books for a good mystery and some light-hearted chuckles, and a mouse strangled with piano wire does not fit either category. Please adjust your tone.*)

(**Note to Editor from Brandy:** *Yes, ma'am. But it did happen. And we really never did solve it.*)

From behind the stand-up piano, Mother rolled out the old schoolroom blackboard she always used to compile her list of suspects, and stood before it, hands clasped beneath her bosom.

"No murder today, darling," she said. "Nor pending theatrical event. No. What I need is your help deciding upon my campaign slogan."

From incident room to campaign headquarters, in a blink!

Mother went on, "Something catchy like *Tippecanoe and Vivian, Too!*"

"Huh?"

She gave me a mildly cross look. "*Tippecanoe and Tyler, Too?* William Henry Harrison's presidential slogan in 1840?" She sighed. "How soon they forget. . . . Tyler was his running mate, and Tippecanoe was a battle Harrison won against the Shawnee nation."

"Okay, first, nobody knows that today; and second, you don't have anything to do with Tippecanoe or Tyler, too; and third, even if you did, bragging about beating Native Americans only works if you're running for sheriff in the 1800s."

Mother's eyes behind the large lenses studied me suspiciously—was I being helpful, or just obstructive?—I'll never tell.

"What other slogans have you come up with?" I asked, realizing my sarcasm had been showing, adding, "And stay away from any presidential ones—you're running for sheriff, remember. *Present-day* sheriff."

"Excellent advice, dear. Although I did rather like Goldwater's *In your heart, you know he's right,* only with a *she.*"

"Maybe so," I said, "but you don't want to remind voters of somebody who lost." Anyway, they might just think, *In your head, you know she's wrong.*

"Good point, dear," Mother replied.

See? I *was* being helpful.

Mother furrowed her brow, then brightened, a lamp with its switch thrown. "How about . . . *A clearer vision for the future!*"

"With those glasses?" Okay, obstructive.

"Qualified, experienced, and dependable?"

"Wouldn't go there." Helpful.

Hands on hips, Mother huffed, "All right, Little Miss Smarty-pants—why don't *you* come up with something?"

So much for Her Darling Girl.

I got up, walked to the blackboard, plucked a piece of white chalk from the wooden lip, then wrote in block letters, *VIVIAN, BORNE TO BE SHERIFF.*

Mother clapped her hands. "Oh, I *do* like that, dear! Very clever. Now, let's talk about promotion."

Since this confab apparently was going to go on for a while, I returned to the bench. Sushi trotted in from the living room and jumped up on my lap. She looked at Mother in a *This-Is-Going-to-Be-Good* fashion.

Mother, resuming her teacherly stance before the blackboard, said, "I have a few notions that I came up with in the middle of the night."

Middle-of-the-night notions were never her best, but at least were frequently entertaining. I waited with bated breath.

With a smile only slightly edged with mania, Mother asked, "Why don't we print leaflets and drop them from an airplane all over town?"

Gulp.

She continued, "And while the plane is up there, it can sky-write my new slogan. Like *Surrender, Dorothy* in *The Wizard of Oz?*"

Pay no attention to the woman behind the curtain.

I took a deep breath, then said slowly, so it would sink in, "I'm pretty sure dropping leaflets from a plane would be considered littering, and you could be fined, which doesn't suggest to the populace that you'd make an ideal sheriff. As for sky-writing, the cost is probably prohibitive."

Mother's face fell like a cake when I opened the oven door too soon. Not that I ever did. Lately.

I shifted on the bench. "By all means, print up leaflets . . . but hand them out instead, you know, wherever you go. Door to door. On street corners. That kind of thing."

Mother made a face. "That's so dull! Not a Vivian Borne–style showstopper."

The last time Mother stopped a show was in *Hello Dolly* when she ("Goodbye!") danced off the stage into the orchestra pit.

She was asking, "What if the plane doesn't sky-write, but merely drags a banner?"

"Again, that depends on the price . . . but it can't be cheap."

Mother frowned, then brightened. "Here's an idea that won't cost too much—you drive me around town while I proclaim my slogan from a bullhorn!"

I shook my head. "Now we'd be disturbing the peace. Look, who's going to pay for all this promotion, once we decide what we can do that won't cost too much, or get you arrested?"

A forefinger was raised in declamatory fashion. "A super PAC?"

"You can't form your own super PAC," I said, "and anyway, who are the big money boys that'll line up to back you?"

"How about a medium PAC?"

"No, not even a teensy-weensy PAC. Mother, you're going to have to get donations the hard way—by going around town and begging your friends for money."

Mother touched a finger to her chin. "I do have friends! Not to mention a few enemies who might contribute, knowing what I have on them."

I sighed. "Blackmail may not be the best way to start your law enforcement career."

She shrugged. "It's worked for many who came before me."

"Be that as it may, the people who donate won't want to see their hard-earned money wasted on any looney-tunes antics like sky-writing."

She sighed. "I suppose you're right, dear. Any suggestions on other ways to raise some campaign funds?"

I thought for a moment. "What about collecting items for a white elephant sale?"

Traditionally a white elephant sale was a step up from the usual garage or rummage varieties because "white elephants" were things of value that had fallen out of favor over time, or were too hard to maintain by an owner but still desirable by others.

Mother exclaimed, "Excellent idea! We could make a good deal of money."

"And look fiscally responsible, trying to self-fund your election, which in turn will encourage supporters to make cash contributions as well."

"Dear, you're a genius," Mother remarked. "What a wonderful campaign manager you'll make!"

"Wait . . . *what?*" I stood, spilling Sushi to the floor like a furry drink. "Let's get this straight. . . . I'm *not* going to be your campaign manager!"

"But you already *are*, dear," Mother said. "You volunteered!"

"I did no such thing."

"It was implied, in the context of all your wise counsel. Anyway, I need you. You can see that. Just look at the unrealistic promotional ideas that *I* came up with without your grounded guidance!"

Her midnight notions really had been pretty bad.

Her expression turned pitifully pleading. "Please say you will? Pretty please?"

My sigh came all the way up from my toes. "Stop. Don't

add *with sugar on top*. I'll do it. I'll hate myself in the morning, but I'll do it."

Mother's pitiful countenance suddenly evaporated. "Thank you, dear. Now, get dressed. Places to go, things to do, people to see."

As she darted past me on her way out, I thought I caught a tiny, smug smile.

Had I just been had?

Had I been played, like one of her smelly old cornets? With nutsy talk of Tippecanoe and leaflets dropping from a plane and sky-writing and a bullhorn and super and medium PACs?

What do you think? (That's rhetorical. We don't need to reopen our conversation.)

Half an hour later, about a quarter to ten, I was behind the wheel of our C-Max, having become the de facto chauffeur in the family since Mother lost her driver's license due to various infractions; she was riding shotgun, while Sushi was left at home holding down the fort.

I've had a few complaints from readers about detailing what Mother and I are wearing in these narratives. If you prefer to think of us as flitting about in the nude, skip the rest of this paragraph. For those of you without dirty minds, I was wearing a floral cotton shirt by Madewell, my favorite DKNY jeans, and a pair of Sam Edelman sandals; Mother was in a pink sweater and matching slacks by Breckenridge, and white shoes custom made to accommodate her painful bunions.

Our destination on this sunny spring morning was the fittingly named Sunny Meadow Manor, an assisted-living/nursing-care facility situated in the country off the bypass—or as Mother calls it, "The Treacherous Bypass," due to the lack of stoplights needed to ensure safe cross-traffic passage.

Mother had always enjoyed visiting nursing homes, and would sometimes drag along a reluctant Brandy, who didn't want to face the final stage of life—especially as depicted by the at-risk patients in wheelchairs lining the hallway, many of whom were forgotten souls.

"Why," I asked, "are we going to Sunny Meadow? You aren't thinking of changing addresses, are you?"

"Unfunny and unkind, dear," Mother replied. "No, my intention is to solicit items from the assisted-living residents for our white elephant sale."

"That doesn't seem very likely to succeed."

"Why do you say that?"

"Well, anybody living there has left their homes behind and most of their belongings."

Mother twisted toward me. "Dear, have you ever been *inside* any of those apartments?"

"Well . . . no."

"If you had, you'd know that the units are indeed rather small, but are usually crammed with more possessions than the residents should ever have brought along with them."

"Not to be crass," I said, "but what makes you think you'll get anything of value?"

"Because, dear, only the very well-off can afford to live in those apartments, with all of the extended services. So they've undoubtedly brought along their *best* things— things that have meaning, but might by now have become burdensome."

"Like a silver tea set," I reasoned, "that needs constant polishing."

"Bingo." Then she lowered her voice: "I really should avoid saying that, since that particular game is almost certainly going on in the commons area."

I took my eyes off the road momentarily. "So your plan

is to weasel these well-off senior citizens out of their best things?"

Mother's laugh was musical, if irritating. "Oh, my, no. They'll practically *beg* me to take them."

I remained skeptical, but in such matters, she was usually right.

I turned off the bypass, then drove west into a countryside of Grant Wood–esque rolling hills comprised of freshly planted fields dotted with the occasional oak or maple tree. Sunny Meadow Manor itself was perched on one of those hills, up a sharp incline, and surrounded by evergreen trees whose boughs gently swayed in the breeze.

I had been to Sunny Meadow Manor several times, having visited Mother there when she was recovering from her double hip replacements—that went back about eight years, when I was still married to Roger and living in a Chicago suburb.

So I was familiar with the layout, which hadn't changed any—the first floor devoted to assisted-living apartments, the second given over to usual nursing home fare, with the third the Alzheimer's Unit. Any higher floor than that would have pearly gates.

As I drove up the incline, Mother said, "Now, I'll do all the talking, dear."

Which I'd planned on, anyway. I was willing to aid but not abet.

I wheeled into the front parking lot, and we exited the car. A wide cement walk took us to double glass doors, which we passed through. To the left was the visitor waiting area, unchanged since Mother's stay: same couches, chairs, and wall prints in soothing pastel colors. The decor did seem a little shopworn now—the fabric on the furniture threadbare in spots, wall prints faded, fake floral arrangements outdated. Still, the section was pleasant enough.

To the right yawned a hallway leading to the administrative wing, muffled voices emanating toward us from various offices. Straight ahead was a reception area consisting of a mahogany desk and chair, the kind of setup a concierge might have in a nice hotel.

No one was behind the desk at the moment, but Mother moved toward it anyway, then bent and picked up a pen tethered to its holder (did the residents here have kleptomaniac relatives?) and proceeded to sign us in to the register.

She had just finished and straightened when a voice rather sternly called, "*Mrs. Borne!*"

We turned.

Rushing toward us from the administrative hallway came a rotund man, pushing fifty, with thinning brown hair, mustache, and wire-framed glasses. He wore a navy business suit, white shirt, plain blue tie, and shiny black shoes. (Or would you prefer to imagine him naked? To each his/her own.)

Planting himself in front of Mother, he said, "Mrs. Borne, I hope you're not on these premises with the intention of collecting *more Vivian-Borne-for-sheriff* signatures from our residents! I've received several complaints from relatives whose loved ones are in the Alzheimer's Unit."

"Oh, goodness, no," Mother gushed. "I've collected all the signatures I needed to file for my candidacy. We're here just to visit." She gestured to me. "This is my daughter, Brandy. Brandy, this is Mr. Burnett—the new managing director of this lovely facility."

"Nice to meet you," I said, and smiled.

Burnett acknowledged my presence with a curt nod. Then he said, "Fine . . . as long as you two really *are* here *just* to visit."

"We are," I said. Which was true in a way.

The manager nodded again, then turned and headed back to the administrative wing, a chugging little engine minus its train.

I gave Mother a hard stare.

"What, dear?" she asked.

"You filed your intent-to-run papers with signatures from *Alzheimer's* patients?"

She shrugged. "Only a few. And only when they really did recognize me. The temptation was to use them more than once."

"That's not funny, Mother."

She patted my arm. "I know, dear. I'll most likely get the disease myself—it runs in the family."

So I had that to look forward to, too, along with bad hips, glaucoma, and bunions. Heredity is such a wonderful thing.

We headed back to the wing of apartments, which totaled twelve in all, where I was soon to discover that Mother had been correct about the residents having brought along too much stuff with them.

Mother's MO for each stop was a cheery ten-minute visit spiced with juicy gossip, followed by a sales pitch for unwanted items for her white elephant sale to finance her campaign for sheriff. Then, when an item was offered, she got an assurance that said item was not on the wish list of any of the giver's relatives.

So as not to take up pages detailing these many visits, here is a recap of what was collected over the next few hours.

Mrs. Rockwell gave Mother a large vintage 1960s sunburst clock by Welby, about two feet across with alternating brass and wood rays, and a black-and-gold face. The reason the woman unloaded the clock: the dial had become too hard for her to read. Interest from relatives:

none. Reason for their rejection: the clock didn't fit their decor; the clock was ugly. (It was. But a discreet check on my cell phone turned up a similar clock for sale on eBay for four hundred and fifty dollars.)

Mrs. Goldstein donated a Louis Vuitton suitcase, circa 1980, medium-sized (the suitcase, not Mrs. Goldstein), brown, with the famous LV logo. Reason for unloading: she didn't travel anymore. Interest from relatives: none. Reason for their rejection: not a complete set; too large for baggage carry-on; too small to use for a long trip; might get stolen at the airport. (eBay value for similar suitcase: between five and eight hundred dollars.)

Mr. Fillmore—to our astonishment—offered to give to the cause his ten-year-old Buick Century with tan leather interior, and mileage of only fifty-plus thousand. Reason for unloading the car: after several near accidents, he had stopped driving, yet was still paying for a parking spot at the facility. Interest from any relatives: none, although a sixteen-year-old grandson who had just gotten his driver's license had expressed interest until he saw the car. Reason for grandson's rejection: he'd never get a girlfriend by driving a "geezer car." (Internet value: three thousand to five thousand dollars.)

Not all of the donations were treasures; some were more in the trash area—like a collection of mostly broken and glued-back-together Hummel figurines, and costume jewelry missing stones. Still, Mother accepted these offerings with the same effusive gratitude as the good stuff.

All in all, it had been a highly successful trip to Sunny Meadow, and I had gotten my daily exercise making multiple trips to and from the C-Max with our loot. (Mr. Fillmore's Buick I would pick up later, as he had to find the title to the car.)

After my final foray outside, I rejoined Mother just after she'd exited the Hummel lady's apartment.

She burbled, "I'd call this a bona fide success, wouldn't you?"

I gave her a simultaneous shrug and nod. "You were right about coming here."

We were heading in the direction of the front entrance when we passed an apartment whose name-plaque read: MRS. HARRIET DOUGLAS.

"Hey, you missed her," I said.

"I didn't miss her, dear."

"She's not a friend, huh?"

"No, Harriet's a *good* friend, but she happens to be the aunt of Deputy Daryl Dugan, my only competition in the race for sheriff."

"Ah," I said, eyebrows flicking up. "Best not to put her on the spot."

"Quite astute, dear."

We were moving away from the apartment's door when it suddenly opened, startling us both into a little dual jump.

Framed in the doorway was a diminutive, plump woman with short, permed white hair and wire-framed glasses. She wore a blue cotton housedress with white bric-a-brac trim, and tan slippers. Standing slightly behind her, a constant companion, was an oxygen tank on wheels, a thin plastic tube running up and around the woman's head to both nostrils.

Harriet clasped her hands and said to Mother, "Oh, good! I've caught you. I was afraid you'd leave without seeing me."

Mother replied, "Harriet, darling, I didn't want to impose upon you because—"

"Yes, yes," the woman interrupted impatiently, "I know why you're here. All of us oldies but goodies text each other. But, please, come in—I'd like a word."

She and her tank moved to allow us passage, and I followed Mother inside.

We were in another cramped living room, which might have been otherwise were it not for all the furniture. The decor was formal in nature: floral chintz couch and matching chair, leather recliner, large tube television, cherry-wood accent table with a Tiffany-style lamp, coffee table, big corner hutch displaying collections of antique plates, glass paperweights, and small crystals (probably Waterford) running on the religious side, like angels and crosses, but with a few animals thrown in.

The air had a strong scent of room freshener, beneath which I detected cigarette smoke, and I hoped Harriet wasn't lighting up around her companion, Mr. Oxygen Tank.

Our hostess said cheerily, "Please, sit."

Mother and I moved to the chintz couch while Harriet took the recliner, parking the tank alongside.

"How *are* you doing with the emphysema, my dear?" Mother asked sympathetically.

"Getting worse all the time, I'm afraid," the woman sighed.

And yet she still smoked.

Harriet seemed to have read my mind, saying, "I only smoke occasionally, when I'm upset, and then I go outside . . . *without* my tank." Our hostess began to cough, and we waited awkwardly for the attack to end.

Then Mother asked, "Was there something in particular that you wanted to see me about, Harriet?"

"Yes," Harriet said, as winded as if she'd just run a race. "I wanted to tell you that—while you and I *are* old friends—I'll be supporting my nephew in his run for sheriff."

"Well, naturally," Mother said. "I wouldn't have expected otherwise." She added graciously, "You must be *very* proud of him."

That was her best piece of acting in some time.

Harriet made a face. ". . . Yes. I guess I am. Blood being

thicker and so on. Still, I *do* cherish our long friendship, Vivian, and so I'd like to quietly, anonymously contribute to your white elephant sale."

Mother smiled, pleased. "How wonderful, dear. And my lips will be forever sealed on the subject."

Harriet gestured to the accent table nearby. "I'd like to give you this Tiffany lamp—it's not an original, of course, but a replica made by the Dale Tiffany Company."

I knew about that company, founded in the late 1970s, and their reproductions were highly respected and sought after. And this particular lamp was exquisite: the glass shade showing ruby red peonies, with green, yellow, and blue accents, and an Art Nouveau bronze base.

I could tell the lamp had Mother excited, too, by the way her eyes sparkled behind her lenses.

I asked, "Are you sure you want to part with it?"

Hand on her heart, Mother said, "Yes, my dear, are you *quite* sure?" But I knew she wanted to kick me.

"I am," Harriet said, nodding to each of us in turn. "I can't read by it, so it's no good to me. And before you ask if anyone in my family wants it, the answer is no."

"Does that include Daryl?" I pressed. I didn't want any further conflict between Deputy Dawg and Mother.

"Especially Daryl," Harriet laughed, which got her coughing again. Then she added, "Daryl and his wife, Candy, have contemporary tastes—besides, I bought the darn lamp, and I can do with it as I please. But if you don't *want* it . . ."

"We want it!" Mother and I said in unison. Perhaps a little too eager.

"Good," Harriet said. "That's settled. Now. There's something *else* I'd like to give Vivian."

Mother and I glanced at each other, in shared wonder about what fabulous treasure might be bestowed upon us next.

Harriet was waving a bony hand at the corner hutch. "It's in the first drawer, right on top."

When Mother started to rise, the woman snapped, "Let Brandy get it—that's what daughters are for."

Brother. Would I be that crabby at her age? Probably, if I were tethered to a tank. Who wouldn't be?

I got off the couch and crossed to the hutch, opened the top drawer, and looked in. Staring back at me was a toothlessly grinning bearded old goofball in a floppy hat.

Gabby Hayes. An autographed photo of the old-time sidekick to cowboy stars in the movies of the thirties, forties, and fifties. The signature had a surprisingly flowing flourish to it.

I picked up the framed black-and-white photo, and turned to Mother and our hostess. "Is *this* what you mean?"

"Yes, yes!" Harriet said. "Give it to your mother!"

I did, then sat back down.

Mother studied the studio still with delight. "Oh, and it's *signed*, too."

"Yes," Harriet said, nodding, "and there's a letter of provenance in the back of the frame."

Mother looked from Gabby to Harriet, whose smiling expressions were similar, although the latter was wearing dentures. "How did you *know* George Hayes was my favorite cowboy character actor?"

Harriet smiled. "You once mentioned to me that you'd learned a lot about acting watching Gabby Hayes display his dramatic skills. It made an impression, and I never forgot it."

Now I could never forget it, either.

Our hostess went on, "But you must *promise* to *keep* the photo, and not sell it in your white elephant sale."

"Why, I wouldn't *dream* of doing such a thing!" Mother exclaimed.

And she meant it, too.

"Good," Harriet said. "Because I got it from Daryl—he has quite an impressive collection of western memorabilia—I don't want him to know that I asked him for it to give it to *you*. It would hurt his feelings. It was from the Judd Pickett collection!"

I said, "Ooooh," as if that meant anything to me.

Mother crossed her heart. "I promise to keep and cherish it, and never to tell."

Antsy to leave, I said, "Well, uh, we should get going. Thank you, Mrs. Douglas, for the lovely lamp."

"And the fabulous photo!" Mother added.

"You're welcome, girls," Harriet replied, then told me where I could find newspapers and a box. Since packing things up was what daughters were good for.

While I wrapped up the lamp, and Mother and Harriet were saying their good-byes, Harriet suddenly said, "There is *one* thing I would love to have from you two."

"What's that, dear?" Mother asked.

"One of your books."

"Which one?"

"Oh, the latest, please," Harriet replied.

"Hardcover or paperback?"

"Hardcover."

"Regular or large print?" Mother asked.

I was holding the box now, and it was getting heavy.

Harriet said, "Large print would be better."

Mother said, "We keep copies in our car for just such requests, and I'll send Brandy back with one."

"Thank you, Vivian. I'll leave the door unlocked."

We made our exit.

In the reception area, the sign-in desk remained vacant, and we didn't bother to sign out because I was holding the heavy, oversize box, and Mother was staring admiringly at Gabby Hayes in her hands, who stared back at her with a rakish, toothless grin.

Outside, the sunny sky had been replaced by ominous dark clouds, the air heavy with the smell of rain soon to come.

In the car, I found a place in the backseat for the box while Mother retrieved our current tome from the trunk. As I hoofed it back to the main entrance, large drops of rain started falling, but I made it to the overhang just before the downpour came.

I stood for a moment watching the deluge, wishing I'd grabbed an umbrella from the car. Then I entered the building, went by the unattended desk, and proceeded down the hallway to Mrs. Douglas's apartment.

I was reaching for the doorknob when an explosion within blew the door off its hinges, and flung me back against the corridor wall like a rag doll.

A Trash 'n' Treasures Tip

Celebrity autographs are easily forged, so buy only from a reputable dealer who will assure its authenticity with a money back guarantee. My heart sank like the *Titanic* when Mother pointed out to me that the signature on my Leo DiCaprio eight-by-ten was spelled *DeCaprio*.

Chapter Two

The Lone Danger

Mother's face slowly came into focus.

"You're going to be all right, dear," she said soothingly.

"Where . . . what . . . ?"

"You are in the emergency room, child, and you *must* lay still. Thrashing about is not an option!"

I couldn't thrash or for that matter turn my head, even if I wanted to, on a table strapped to a board as I was, a brace around my neck.

I began to ask what had happened, but then it came suddenly back: the explosion, the door to the apartment flying off its hinges like an Oz-size tornado had taken it, and my body being violently hurled against the wall.

"And . . . Harriet?" I asked.

Mother shook her head slowly, wearing the matter-of-fact expression she always does in the face of tragedy.

"I'm afraid she's dead, dear," she said. Then, as if to herself, "I *do* hope she'd planned on cremation, when the time came."

A male doctor in a white smock materialized next to Mother like an efficient ghost.

"Excellent, she's awake," he said in an East Indian accent, his ID tag sharing an impossibly long name, consonants struggling with vowels for domination.

Did you know that when an Indian male marries, he takes his wife's last name? (I don't know why I mentioned that. I don't even know why I know.)

The doctor peered down at his patient. "You've had a concussion, Miss Borne, so I've ordered a CT scan to make sure there's been no injury to your head."

"My left shoulder really hurts," I told him.

"No doubt—it's quite bruised. We'll have an X-ray of that as well, but no bones appear to have been broken."

Two female interns drew a gurney alongside my table, then carefully slid me-on-my-board onto it, like a slice of pizza onto a plate.

As the pair began to wheel me away, Mother chirped, "Have a safe journey, dear!" *Don't forget to write!*

In a blindingly white room that looked every bit as sterile as it no doubt was, I was transferred to a padded table attached to a machine that looked like a huge donut. Unstrapped now, neck brace removed, I received a few instructions from a technician and then the table began to move, and my head disappeared into the donut hole.

The procedure took about half an hour, and when I was gurneyed back to the ER, Mother was having a conversation with Serenity's chief of police, Tony Cassato.

Tony was also my on-again, off-again boyfriend, now (I'm pleased to say) on-again. Our boomeranging relationship had nothing to do with discord, rather a series of interruptions over the past few years caused by various out-of-our-control events (**spoiler alert**) including a brief reconciliation with my ex-husband, a New Jersey mob contract sending Tony into WITSEC, and the sudden appear-

ance of a wife Tony thought he had divorced. You know—
little things (**end spoiler alert**).

But now we were happily back on track again.

Tony, wearing his typical nonuniform uniform—navy
jacket, light blue shirt, blue-and-white striped tie, and gray
slacks—broke away from Mother and strode toward me-
on-my-transport. In his late forties, barrel-chested, bull-
necked, with a square jaw, bulbous nose, and graying hair
at the temples, the chief watched as the interns redeposited
me onto the examination table. Then he took my hand—
how such a rough paw could be so gentle is one of the
great wonders of nature.

"How are you feeling, sweetheart?" he asked, steely
eyes showing concern.

Much better, hearing him calling me *sweetheart* without
caring who heard.

I said, "Sore, but okay."

He nodded. "You got lucky. If you'd been two seconds
earlier, well . . ." He shuddered.

"All great comedians have great timing," I said with a
smile, as the neck brace was eased off me by a male nurse.
"You've been to the scene?"

"No. Sheriff's jurisdiction."

"Oh, right." Sunny Meadow was outside city limits. I
looked over at Mother, who was keeping a respectful distance. "Your favorite civilian assistant must have been disappointed, not being able to get any information out of you."

"Every negative has its positive side," he said with a
smile and glance toward Mother.

The doctor with the warring consonants and vowels approached.

"Well, Miss Borne, I've had a look at the X-rays."

"Can you confirm the presence of a brain?"

He didn't smile at that, so if you didn't either, that's
okay. Timing isn't everything.

He merely said, "You do indeed have a brain, and it appears to be functioning normally. No swelling."

Mother sidled up to the doctor, actual concern breaking through her matter-of-fact face. "What about the poor dear's shoulder?"

"No broken bones," he assured her. "But it will be sore for a while. Nothing that over-the-counter pain medication can't handle.

"Can you give me something stronger?" I asked.

"If the discomfort gets worse, I'll consider that . . . but try the other first."

What good was it, getting nearly blown up, when they wouldn't give you the good drugs? But doctors had gotten stingy with dispensing narcotics, so I didn't press it. Besides, there were some opioid tablets in our medicine cabinet left over from Mother's double hip replacement.

The doctor was saying, "I'll sign your release papers and then you can go."

I thanked him, and he and his endless name went off to attend to another patient.

I asked Tony to help me sit up, and he did, asking, "Do you need a ride home?"

I looked at Mother. "Do we?"

"Someone from Sunny Meadow drove me here in our car," she claimed. Of course, it was likely she'd driven herself, despite her lack of license, but she appeared to be actress enough to get that past the chief.

Tony's cell phone rang, and he moved away to answer it.

Eyes narrowed, I asked Mother, "Is that true?"

"Is *what* true, dear?" she replied with a lift of the chin and a mild smile that shouted innocence.

"*You* know!" I whispered. "Someone *really* drove you?"

She patted my arm. "What difference does it make now? There were no incidents."

Like knocking over a mailbox or cutting through a cornfield.

"You're going home," she said. "You should be happy."

"Someday you're going to get caught with your pants down."

"Well, dear, it won't be the first time, and I seem to have survived. Shhhhh . . . here comes you-know-who."

Tony rolled over like a friendly tank. "Brandy, I've got to leave—duty calls and so on. Want me to stop by later?"

"Thanks, but I'm going right to bed and taking as much Tylenol as I dare." His brave smile prompted me to add, "But I'd love to have dinner some night this week."

Mr. Serious gave me a rare wink. "Sounds like just the right medicine."

With a quick kiss on the forehead, and a nod to Mother, he started out, then paused at the door. "Oh, Vivian?"

"Yes, Chiefie?"

"Who exactly was it from Sunny Meadow who drove you over in your car? Does he or she need a ride back, maybe?"

His smile was a cute little threat.

A forefinger to her cheek, Mother said, "I didn't get the name, and I believe someone followed us here, to take my driver back, whoever he was. Yes, I'm sure of it!"

"I'm sure, too, Vivian," Tony said, and was gone.

Mother beamed at me. "I think he bought that."

"Oh, definitely."

Midafternoon, Mother and I arrived home from the ER—I was doing the driving, still shaken up but, unlike Mother, legally licensed—and Sushi was so happy to see us she piddled in the entryway on the wood floor. *Piddled* sounds cuter than it was.

"I'll clean it up, dear," Mother said. "Mustn't put a strain on the patient!" She went off to the kitchen to get the necessary supplies as I reflected on just how, and how long, I might milk my accident.

Seeing no reason to put Sushi out now, I walked surprisingly steadily across the Persian rug to sit on a hard antique Queen Anne sofa. Since forever, I had been lobbying for a more comfortable couch, but Mother would have none of it—modern furniture just didn't cut the muster with the all-Victorian living room decor.

(**Mother to Brandy:** *Pardon the interruption, dear, but the correct expression is* cut the mustard.)

(**Brandy to Mother:** *How can you cut mustard?*)

(**Mother to Brandy:** *The reference is in determining heat and piquancy in making the condiment.*)

(**Brandy to Mother:** *Where does muster come in?*)

(**Mother to Brandy:** *Nowhere, in this instance. But when something is adequately done, it "passes muster."*)

(**Brandy to Mother:** *What's the difference?*)

(**Mother to Brandy:** *Essentially, the two sayings mean the same thing, albeit in a different fashion.*)

(**Brandy to Mother:** *Then why can't I interchange them?*)

(**Editor to Brandy and Vivian:** *Ladies?*)

(**Vivian to Editor:** *With all due respect, this as an excellent opportunity to explain these two much-maligned and misunderstood expressions to the masses.*)

(**Editor to Vivian:** *If you continue to lecture your readers, they will hardly collect into anything resembling a mass. Please move on.*)

(**Brandy to Editor:** *Already have.*)

Sushi, who'd always been sensitive to my moods, jumped onto the couch and gazed at me with large brown eyes. Not long ago those eyes had seen nothing, due to her diabetes, but we'd sprung for her surgery out of a storage-locker windfall a while back.

"It's okay, girl," I said, petting her soft, long fur until she curled up beside me.

Mother, cleanup duty done, joined me on the couch, sitting primly, knees together, hands on knees. "And what would you like for dinner, dear? Your wish, my command."

"I'm not hungry."

"You should eat *something* after what you've endured. . . ."

"I just want a shower and enough energy to crawl into bed."

Sushi suddenly lifted her head and emitted a low growl, drawing our attention out the picture window, where a paunchy, tan-uniformed individual was climbing out of the driver's side of a patrol car, as if every muscle and bone in his body pained him. But more likely it was the thought of confronting Vivian Borne that gave Sheriff Pete Rudder a pain, and in one specific place at that.

I groaned—I was in no shape, or mood, for this. "You can talk to him if you want, Mother, but tell the man I've gone to sleep. Say it was doctor's orders!"

She twisted toward me. "It's best to answer his questions now, dear—I can't handle this one."

"You always handle this sort of thing!"

"Only when I'm the one nearly blown up. You should speak now, while the event is fresh in your mind. I'll be right here at your side!"

"Oh, I know you will be. You just want to pump the poor man for information!"

Her eyes were wide and slightly magnified behind her big-framed glasses. "Don't *you* want to know what he knows? After all, you were nearly killed! That doesn't happen every day, dear, even to us."

The doorbell rang, and Mother flounced from the couch to answer it. I closed my eyes and shivered.

After a muffled exchange at the door, she stepped aside and Rudder—looking perfectly pressed, gun holstered at his side—strode in, tall, imposing, reminding me of the older Randolph Scott (if I wasn't wearing my contacts) while Mother always said Rudder looked like a late-in-life John Wayne (if she squinted). While this ongoing disagreement was unlikely ever to be settled, I will concede that Rudder did walk kind of sideways like the Duke.

Mother addressed our guest in an embarrassingly formal way, stopping just short of the pretentious faux English accent she sometimes lapsed into.

"*Do* have a seat, won't you, please, Sheriff Rudder?" She gestured theatrically to a Queen Anne needlepoint chair that was too small for a man half his stature.

"Coffee, tea . . . ?" the hostess with the mostest asked, her flirtatious smile seeming to add, ". . . me?" Only in Mother's case it would be "*moi.*"

"Nothing, Vivian, thank you," he said, and managed to perch on the edge of the needlepoint chair's cushion.

Meanwhile, Mother fluttered to the larger needlepoint chair, with arms, and sat as regally as the chair's namesake on her throne. (Forgive my ambiguity—was I referring to Mother or Queen Anne? Or does it really matter?)

For all Mother's butter-wouldn't-melt welcoming of the sheriff, the two of us had a longtime, contentious relationship with Rudder, she and I having solved several murder cases that were on his patch. Still, he may have held some small admiration—however grudgingly—for our sleuthing abilities.

Rudder addressed me, "I understand you had quite the close call, young lady."

I nodded, smiling a little. I'm just at the age where being called "young lady" doesn't sound so bad.

"Tell me all about it," he said, looking like he might fall off that chair and suffer worse injuries than I had.

"Not much to say, really," I replied. "Mother and I spent the late morning at Sunny Meadow collecting items for a white elephant sale to fund her campaign . . . for sheriff?"

"Yes, I know," he said dryly.

"Mrs. Douglas was the last person we saw about that."

Rudder's eyes traveled to Mother. "Rather strange, don't you think, Vivian? Soliciting help from the aunt of your political rival?"

The Queen leaned forward on her throne. "How *is* Deputy Dugan taking his loved one's untimely demise?"

"Rather hard, really," the sheriff said, eyebrows lifting, lowering. "They were very close, more like mother and son." He paused. "Daryl was over in West Liberty, dealing with a domestic dispute, when the accident happened."

Had he given us the deputy's whereabouts to head off Mother's snooping? And was that why he'd emphasized how close aunt and nephew had been? He shouldn't have bothered—Mother never spares the bereaved from her suspect list.

Rudder was asking, "Could we, uh, get back to my question, ladies?"

Now I was a "lady." No "young" attached.

"Certainly," Mother said with a shrug. "Harriet donated something to the sale out of our long-standing friendship, nonetheless making it *clear* her nephew would be getting her vote."

"Then what happened?"

My turn to shrug. "Then we left and went out to the car, where I got a book of ours Mrs. Douglas requested. When I got back to her apartment door . . ."

"Ka-*boom!*" Mother said.

The sheriff almost tumbled from the tiny chair. But he managed to ask, "Did she happen to be smoking during your visit?" The question was for either of us.

Mother took it. "Good gracious no! I would never have allowed it. She was on oxygen! Anyway, it wouldn't have been good for her."

"Especially with the oxygen," I said.

"But," Rudder said, his lifted eyebrow staying that way for a while, "she *could* have lit a cigarette while waiting for you to bring her that book—rather than going outside without the tank, which I understand is Sunny Meadow's policy."

"That seems a possibility," Mother granted. "And the bouquet of cigarette smoke *was* present in her apartment."

"But that doesn't mean she lighted up there," I said. "You know how smoke clings to clothing—she could have got that from smoking inside or out."

The sheriff sighed, nodded, then suddenly stood and announced, "Well, girls, that's all for now."

And now I was a girl. Better than a lady!

The Queen flew to her feet, with a decided lack of royal dignity. "You're not *leaving*?"

"I'm done."

"But *I'm* not!" she protested, eyes and nostrils flaring like a rearing horse. She began ticking things off on her fingers. "I want to know what agencies are investigating the accident besides the local fire marshal. Will the *state* fire marshal be involved? What about the Bureau of Alcohol, Tobacco, Firearms, and Explosives? And Homeland Security? Certainly, the company that manufactured the oxygen tank will want to know that its product wasn't defective. Additionally, any insurance company Harriet had coverage with will *insist* on being involved." Mother had stopped only because she ran out of breath, if not fingers.

Rudder's eyes were lidded and his smile was just vaguely nasty. "I see no need or reason to share any of that information with you, Vivian."

"Really? No need? No reason?" Mother drew herself up. "Aren't political candidates given confidential briefings?"

He chuckled, genuinely amused. "You're not running for president of the United States—you don't get CIA briefings when you run for sheriff."

Mother put her hands on hips, like Superman at the start of the old-time TV show, lacking only the flapping cape. "But that gives Deputy Dugan the inside *track*, the upper hand as it were—how is that fair? How will the League of Women Voters feel about *that*?"

"He's not involved in the investigation," Rudder told her. "And neither is the League of Women Voters."

I found the first part of that interesting. "Dugan is excluded—why? Because Harriet was his aunt?"

Rudder's eyes went to me. "No, it's because *I'm* still sheriff—for a few more months, anyway. I'm handling the investigation personally. He has his routine duties to take care of."

And without a good-bye, or even a nod, he left, quickly, almost as if making his escape.

Mother stood at the window watching the sheriff until he pulled away from the curb.

When she remained frozen, I asked, "What?"

"*What* what?"

"What's going on in your devious mind?"

Mother turned, frowning, though not taking offense by my characterization of her thinking apparatus. "Don't you think it odd, dear, that he didn't take the opportunity to disparage my run for sheriff?"

I squinted. "Yes," I admitted. "You would think he'd have given you at least one good zinger. Like when he said, 'You're not running for president . . . you're running for sheriff,' he could have added 'heaven help us,' or worse."

"Well, he wasn't entirely devoid of rudeness, but I am surprised that my aspirations to the job from which he's departing weren't in *some* fashion denigrated."

My behind had gone to sleep and I wanted the rest of me to join it. Rising from the hard couch, I announced, "I'm going upstairs—don't wake me until morning unless another explosion is imminent."

"All right, dear. Sleep tight!"

Mother had stopped adding, "And don't let the bedbugs bite," after she'd brought home an infested patchwork pillow from a garage sale.

Upstairs, I took a hot shower, got into some comfy pajamas, and—in my Art Deco bedroom with its 1930s matching bird's-eye maple furniture—crawled under the sheets. I was about to drop off when my cell phone on the nightstand pinged.

Want some company? Tony texted.
Thanks, but I'm in bed, I texted back.
Wish I could join you.
I smiled. That was about as racy as Tony got.
Me, too. Call me tomorrow. Love you!

Someone in history must have slept more soundly than I did that night, but I don't know who it would have been. Maybe Queen Anne.

The following morning, Tuesday, I felt rested enough to work with Mother at our antiques shop, Trash 'n' Treasures, located in a turn-of-the-last-century, two-story white clapboard house downtown, where the business district ended and a residential area began to climb East Hill.

Before we bought the vacant property, it was known around town as "the murder house," after a notorious ax killing happened there (*Antiques Chop*—okay, so our titles aren't subtle). Mother had no qualms about moving

in, and my qualms were somewhat eased after Father
O'Brien blessed the house, even if we weren't Catholic. (By
the way, should these parenthetical asides be getting on
your nerves, best buckle up—they're not going to disap-
pear anytime soon.)

The house worked well to showcase our wares—we had
arranged everything according to the room in which the
antique or collectible might normally have been found.
Living room furnishings in the living room, dining room
items in the dining room, ditto the kitchen, bedrooms (one
a nursery with children's things), hall linen closet, and
bathroom with claw-foot tub. The attic held old junk,
from ancient steamer trunks to salvaged doors, and the
basement contained "mantiques," like old tools and beer
signs.

Sometimes Mother and I would have an argument over
which room should be a new old item's home, like the oil
painting of a vase of flowers, which I thought would go better (and sell better) in the dining room, while she wanted it
in the living room. When such squabbles happen, we let
Sushi decide—whichever of the two rooms she goes into
first gets the item. So far, Soosh has always gone with my
pick. Perhaps the little angel has good instincts . . . or
maybe she just knows how to sniff out a little doggie biscuit somebody had hidden. . . .

Customers, by the way, were always telling us that their
trip to Trash 'n' Treasures was like visiting a favorite el-
derly relative (hopefully one who hadn't been dispatched
with an ax). Maybe that was because, in the kitchen, free
goodies were always waiting—hot coffee and cookies
baked fresh every day in the working stove, their aroma
wafting throughout the house.

At the moment I was seated at the small checkout
counter in the foyer, making sales entries in the computer.
Sushi, who always came to work with us, slept behind me

in a leopard-print doggie bed on the floor. Mother was in the living room, dusting.

When the little bell above the front door tinkled, signaling a customer, I looked up from the screen, while Sushi gave a sharp bark from her bed, just in case I hadn't heard it.

As long as we'd been in business—and since having a cable reality show, short-lived though it was—all kinds of folks ventured to our shop . . . but none surprised me more than the person who just walked in.

"Good morning, Deputy," I said.

Daryl Dugan was about forty, just under six feet, with short dark hair, chiseled features, and muscles stretching the fabric of his tan shirt. What kept him from being a hunk in my book were close-set eyes that gave him a mildly dim-witted look. The extent of what I knew about him was that he'd been in the service before entering law enforcement, and had recently married a woman my age, who had two ex-husbands.

The deputy approached the counter. "You're all right?"

"Doing fine, thanks."

He let out some air. "I'm glad," he said, with seeming sincerity.

"I'm so sorry about your aunt," I replied, meaning it. "She was a sweetheart." Even if she had ordered me around like a top sergeant.

He nodded. "She was very special to me."

"This kind of thing . . . it's always hard."

This kind of thing? What was I saying? Was it usual for a room at a nursing home to blow sky high?

Dugan shifted his stance. "Sheriff mentioned Aunt Harriet had given you something of hers."

Uh-oh. "She did. We asked her if she was sure no family member wanted it, and she said—"

He silenced me with an upraised palm, as if taking the oath in court. "I understand. It's just that, well, everything was destroyed in the explosion and fire, and I might like to have it to remember her by. I'd pay you for it, certainly. What was it?"

Mother, who'd almost certainly been listening from the living room, popped in. "It was a lamp, Mr. Dugan, a replica of an original Tiffany. Do you know of what I'm speaking?"

The deputy nodded. "Yes. Not exactly the kind of family memento I was hoping for. Was that all she gave you?"

"That's all that was in the box," Mother said.

Which wasn't a lie, because she'd hand-carried the photo of Gabby Hayes. Such nuances were important to her. And since the deputy collected western stuff, he might have asked for that back. And Mother did have a thing about Gabby Hayes. . . .

Mother moved behind the counter to stand next to me. "So do you want the lamp or not?" she asked Dugan, rather bluntly.

He nodded. "It was my aunt's after all—I'll pay for it, as I told Brandy. But I'd appreciate it if I could do that now." A wry smile. "Would be a little embarrassing to go to your sale and be seen giving money to your campaign."

"Four hundred dollars," Mother said.

I gave her a gentle kick.

"Oh, I'm just a sentimental soul," Mother said, reaching a leg up to rub where I'd kicked. "Make it two hundred."

She raised a hand to stop me from kicking her again.

The deputy was frowning. "Well, uh . . ."

"Make it fifty," Mother said, "between friendly rivals."

I said sweetly, "*Of course* the lamp is yours." I turned to Mother and gave her a look that would have frozen water. "Where is it?"

Her magnified eyes behind the impossibly large glasses threw daggers at me. "In the back. With the other white elephant items."

My sweet tone took on sour edges. "Why don't you get it, Mother, since you know right where it is?"

After she'd left in a huff, I said to Dugan, "I need to talk to you in private—will you be home tonight around seven?"

He reared back just a little. "Ah . . . I could be. What's this about, Brandy?"

"I'd rather not get into it here. *Will* you be there?"

"Yeah, okay. Sure. Glad to."

"Good. Where do you live?"

He told me.

Mother appeared with the lamp, still packed in the box the deputy's aunt had provided.

He took it, thanked us for our generosity, then left.

For a long moment after the door had closed, Mother said nothing. Then, angrily, she said, "That money is going to come out of *your* end."

"Look, a little goodwill coming in to this election can't hurt. Besides, no doubt you'll spread the story of your magnanimous gesture all over town."

Mother harrumphed. "You mean *your* magnanimous gesture." She suddenly softened. "Well, perhaps it will generate some good karma. You were right to give him that lamp. And we'll both absorb the loss."

"We didn't pay anything for it!"

"But we'll never know what it might have raised for the campaign, will we? Anyway, I have a way for you to pay me back."

"I don't owe you anything."

"Of course you do. Don't forget, I have a stump speech to give at two o'clock this afternoon. And you will be there, cheering me on!"

The Serenity League of Women Voters had invited Mother to address them after their luncheon at the Grand Queen Hotel.

While Mother returned to her dusting, I sat feeling guilty about my clandestine meeting tonight with her foe.

A little guilty.

A *Trash 'n' Treasures Tip*

There are no set rules for a white elephant sale. Sometimes an admission is charged, other times attendance is free; some have set prices, others are auction format. Knowing what guidelines apply before going will make your experience more satisfying and fun. Mother is often on top of such guidelines, having muscled her way onto the committee that makes the rules.

Chapter Three

Paint Your Bandwagon

Leaving Sushi behind in the shop with kibbles and water and her comfy bed, Mother and I departed at a quarter to two, pausing on the stoop long enough for her to tape a note she had written to the locked front door:

CLOSED FOR STUMP SPEECH
LEAGUE OF WOMEN VOTERS
2 PM, GRAND QUEEN HOTEL BALLROOM
ALL WOMEN* WELCOME
(*includes transgenders but not transvestites)
(the latter welcome at Trash 'n' Treasures always!)
(The former, too.)

Okay, so it wasn't a note—more like a sheet. And, no, I didn't try to stop her; I had a bigger concern at the moment: what Mother was going to say to the good women of Serenity.

Earlier, when I had asked to see her speech, she blithely told me she'd written nothing down—it was all "safely and securely ensconced in the old noodle." Now, on the three-block walk to the hotel, I tried to get her to un-ensconce it and share whatever exactly was rattling around in there.

"Dear," Mother replied, "I don't know precisely what words will come trippingly off my tongue. I am well-versed in improv, as you well know. Further, I am a *thespian*—more at ease in front of an audience than most are in the privacy of their own homes."

True. But the words spoken on stage at our local community theater came from the likes of Shakespeare, Ibsen, Wilde, and Coward. Or at least John Patrick, author of *Everybody Loves Opal* and its five sequels.

As the hotel came into view, Mother paused to soliloquize. "Behold the Grand Queen in all her splendor! And to think she could have been lost."

Two decades ago, the eight-story Victorian edifice, situated on a bank of the Mississippi, had been slated for demolition, when the wealthy publisher of the *Serenity Sentinel* bought the building and gave it a much-needed three-million-dollar face-lift. The publisher also boldly implemented a (then) innovative concept of guest rooms in the form of fantasy suites. People came from far and wide, and still do, to experience the way-out moon room complete with space-capsule bed, or decadent Grecian playground with unlikely hot tub, or to spend the night on the bridge of the starship *Enterprise* (or the newer *Next Generation* bridge, so popular with bald bridegrooms).

But a few suites had gotten the ax after giving guests nightmares instead of fantasies—like the too-realistic claustrophobia-inducing submarine suite, also responsible for heart palpitations when the "dive" horn (*auugh-OOGAH!*) unexpectedly bleated. Also controversial were the captain's rustic pirate-ship cabin with its seasick-inducing motorized floor, and Tarzan's tree house, from the bed in which tumbled an acrobatic honeymooning couple, breaking various limbs—tree *and* human.

Mother and I entered the hotel via a side door, then followed a marbled hallway to an elevator, which took us up to the third floor. Her chin high, her smile confident, her magnified eyes half-lidded, Mother was obviously not at all nervous about this new theatrical venue.

As the doors swished open, we were greeted with boisterous after-luncheon chatter accompanied by the clanking and clinking of glasses and dishes as waitstaff cleared tables. We stepped into the elegantly appointed ballroom, its decor reflecting a recent remodel, yet in keeping with the hotel's Victorian-era history.

A few things remained original—the shimmering center ceiling chandelier, for example, and beautiful dark oak wainscoting. The iris-patterned wallpaper by nineteenth-century English artisans Morris and Crane had also been salvaged, its faded beauty only enhanced by the newer touches.

Before us stretched at least a hundred women ranging from early twenties to late eighties, seated at dozens of linen-covered tables seating four, enjoying after-dinner coffee along with assorted petits fours. A similarly linen-dressed head table with a podium at its center stretched along the far wall where windows looked out on the sparkling river.

Mrs. Snydacker, president of the league, came from that table to rush up to us. She was a handsome woman in her fifties, though an overzealous plastic surgeon had done her no favors; she wore a none too subtle patriotic ensemble—navy dress, red scarf, white shoes.

"I was afraid you'd be *late!*" the woman said irritably.

This had been directed at Mother, who calmly intoned, "My dear, I've *never* been late to a performance."

Apparently, the opening night of *Everybody Loves Opal* had slipped her mind. Remember the earlier reference to

Mother driving through a cornfield? That occurred when, trying to make curtain, she had collided with a combine. (And as I indicated, not every play Mother appeared in was by Shakespeare, Ibsen, Wilde, or Coward.)

Mrs. Snydacker escorted Mother to the head table where a microphone awaited on a podium. I stayed put at the rear, safely out of range for flying petits fours, should the audience become riled by her speech. Everybody may love Opal, but everybody in Serenity definitely did not love Vivian.

The league's president tapped the microphone, then said, in a too loud, slightly shrill voice, "Ladies, I'd like to introduce Vivian Borne, who is running for county sheriff."

And she stepped aside, giving Mother a slight nod and slighter smile.

Even from the back of the room, I could tell Mother was miffed by the miserly introduction. But, ever the eager performer, the diva smiled graciously and took her place, standing straight, standing tall. Maybe not as tall as Buford Pusser, but tall enough.

In the overly formal tone she reserved for impressing people—thankfully absent any trace of her mock-British accent—Mother began, "I'd like to thank the Serenity League of Women Voters, and Mrs. Snydacker in particular, for allowing me to speak to you this afternoon."

From somewhere—like Bugs Bunny producing an anvil—Mother conjured a sheaf of paper.

She *did* have her speech written down, the big fibber!

"But before I begin my oration," Mother said, "or as we say in the Midwest, my *spiel* . . ."

Mother smiled and waited for a laugh that never came. I swear I heard a cricket.

She continued, unswayed: "In the spirit of complete transparency, I should like to produce several documents."

Say what?

She held up one paper. "*This* is my birth certificate, which proves without a doubt that I was born in America—the, uh, smear at the birth date appears to have been an unfortunate slip-up on the registrar's part—still, there can be no doubt whatsoever that I am indeed a U.S. citizen."

I had a hunch I wasn't the only one in this crowd whose mouth had dropped open. But all I saw were the backs of heads. I was pretty sure the front view was the audience at *Springtime for Hitler* during the opening song.

Mother waved another paper, like Joe McCarthy producing a list of Commies in government. "And *this* is a copy of my recent physical, showing that I am in excellent, A-plus condition! Blood pressure and cholesterol within normal range, no heart disease, or diabetes. Though, uh . . . full disclosure! I *do* have bothersome bunions—but a little pad on them seems to do the trick."

A smattering of laughter.

Okay, I thought. *Better. She wasn't joking, but at least she got a laugh. . . .*

"Concerning my e-mails," Mother continued in earnest, leaning over the podium, "I will readily make them available to all and sundry who are interested. I have nothing to hide—no classified information there!"

Ripples of laughter. Again, not really a joke, but she was winning them over in spite of herself.

"Plus, for your consideration, I will also make public my tax returns. Unfortunately my records only go back three years. . . . I assure you no attempt to conceal anything from the public is my intention! The earlier ones were simply lost when our house blew up."

Louder laughter. But I promise you that was no joke—the house really did blow up! Of course, Mother just had it rebuilt from the original plans in our safe deposit box.

"And finally, there is *no* Vivian Borne Foundation . . . no oil-painting portrait of me bought with foundation money, and no pay-for-play deals between myself and any foreign entity."

Raucous laughter.

Obviously, the audience figured Mother was poking fun at a certain presidential election. But, by her dawning look of puzzlement at these reactions, I could tell she'd been serious. A lesser female showman would have been thrown. Not Mother.

She embraced it. Her head went back and her smile was endless, wider than the Cheshire cat's. "It's nice to see we can at long last laugh at that most contentious time!"

Enthusiastic applause.

When the clapping had died down, Mother launched into her extemporaneous speech. "If elected sheriff of this great county, I vow to replace the department's old communications system with a new state-of-the-art one, improving both efficiency and accuracy." She raised a finger. "And this can be done with *no* cost to the taxpayer!"

Skeptical murmurs.

"As many of you know, I have been most successful in obtaining grants for various community causes, such as the new wing for the library, and funds to improve conditions at the shelter for battered women."

True. Grant givers quickly learned that Mother was relentless in her quest for free money and had learned to just pony up.

Mother continued, "I will also improve the department by adding a third deputy, which will reduce errors due to fatigue, *and* bolster morale among the staff. This, too, can be accomplished with no increase to the budget. As it stands now, the county is paying two deputies overtime to fill the needs of the community, which is *not* financially efficient. Why not use the overtime cost to add another position?"

Positive murmurs now were accompanied by nodding

of heads. The ladies were liking what they were hearing. And, I had to admit, so—astonishingly—was I.

"And finally," Mother said, "I'd like to see a better relationship between the sheriff's department and the community. I'm not saying that conditions are poor—Sheriff Rudder has done a commendable job. But there's always room for improvement. Remember, gaining the public's trust has always been—and always will be—an integral part of law enforcement."

Ebullient applause.

Wow, I thought. *That wasn't bad! That was really kind of . . . good.*

"Thank you," Mother said graciously, nodding, bowing, glancing here and there as if expecting someone to rush the stage with an armload of flowers. "Now, I'm happy to take questions from the audience, should anyone have any."

A hand shot up—Frannie Phillips, one of Mother's gal pals, probably enlisted as a shill.

"Mrs. Borne," the woman said in a loud voice that seemed to acknowledge the older, more hard-of-hearing among us, "isn't it true that you have already solved many baffling cases for the sheriff's department?"

"Well, now . . ." Mother demurred, shifting her stance, wearing her modesty like an orchid on a prom dress. "To be perfectly honest, and answering your query with some reluctance . . . that is correct. I have always been happy to share credit with both the Serenity Police Department and the county sheriff on these occasions. What does it matter that I have exposed something like a dozen murderers! Seeing justice served is more important to me than taking any credit."

Let's give that Five Pinocchios, or whatever is the maximum nose growth on the lying scale. I refer to the latter statement only—she really has brought a dozen or so murderers to justice. Or anyway she and I have.

Another hand shot up, Alice Hetzler, also a gal pal—really Shill-O-Rama here at the League of Women Voters this afternoon!

"Ms. Borne, what would you say to someone who would question your age and fitness to be sheriff?"

While not exactly a softball question, it was smart of Mother to address that issue now.

"Age is but a number," Mother responded with airy certainty. "What really matters is a person's ability to do the job, and I certainly have the stamina to become sheriff. As far as fitness is concerned—I will post my medical report on line. Besides, there seems to be a goodly and ever-growing number—if you'll pardon the pun—of law enforcement professionals who could stand to drop a pound or two."

That brought some chuckles.

A younger woman I didn't recognize put her hand up; her hair was short and dark and her suit was gray with a black silk blouse—a professional among the ladies who lunch.

"Leslie Hackett," she said. *"Des Moines Register."*

"Ah," Mother replied. "It's nice to see a member of the fourth estate—and from our state's capital!—interested in our little election. What is your question, Ms. Hackett?"

"Isn't it *true* that while apprehending a murderer at the county fairgrounds a few years back you *purposely* burned down the historic grandstand?"

To Mother's credit she didn't flinch. "That was an unfortunate accident. Burning down the grandstand, that is. Capturing a murderer was wholly intentional."

Four Pinocchios. Cornered by a killer, Mother set a very intentional fire to attract help; but I don't think she intended the old wooden structure to go up in flames.

"Besides," Mother went on, "out of the ashes came a brand-new grandstand. A win-win if you ask me. . . . You're welcome, Serenity!"

But Ms. Hackett wasn't finished. "And isn't it a *fact* that you've been incarcerated multiple times?"

"I wouldn't call two stints in the pokey 'multiple,' dear," Mother replied, brow furrowed, smile smirky.

"Once for falsely admitting to a murder . . ."

Mother cut in. "Only a temporary admission, to protect someone else from being charged—someone who was *innocent.*"

Me.

". . . and again for breaking and entering someone's home."

"Who was a *murderer*," Mother said, adding, "Different case, by the way." As if that took the onus off.

"One would think," the reporter said, "these . . . shall we say, vigilante actions would *disqualify* you as a candidate for sheriff."

"My record has been expunged," Mother huffed. "*If* you'd bothered to check the facts."

Half a Pinocchio: the charge for false confession was dropped; the break-in really was expunged, but only after she (and I, as her accessory) spent a month in the county jail.

Time to bring the Q & A to an end. This wasn't accomplishing anything good, except maybe selling a few books locally. I twirled a finger in the air, catching Mother's eye.

"Oh, my," she exclaimed, "look at the time. I didn't mean to go on so long. Again, I'd like to thank the Serenity League of Women Voters for inviting me this afternoon. And remember, ladies—vote for me, Vivian Borne—*born to be sheriff!*"

She left the podium in haste, to a smattering of applause, and we made a quick exit.

In the elevator Mother's sneer had some snarl in it. "Why didn't that young woman stick to her own beat? She just came here to make trouble, and make a name for herself at my expense."

"Is any of what you said true?" I asked.

"Of course! She just came to make trouble!"

"No. In your speech, I mean. *Is* there a grant to pay for a new communications system?"

Her shrug oozed unconcern. "I'm sure there's one somewhere."

I reached for the buttons and stopped the elevator.

I narrowed my eyes at her and leaned in. "What about adding a new deputy, virtually cost free?"

She shrugged again. "Well, I haven't really done the math on that."

My squint gave way to climbing eyebrows. "Mother, you can't go around making campaign promises you can't keep!"

Her smile was a blossom of motherly love for a backward child.

"Dear," she said, "can you really be so naive? Nobody *really* believes a candidate will keep his—or in this case, *her*—promises. Now let's get Sushi and go home . . . my bunions are *killing* me!"

And she started the elevator.

So much for her A-plus health report.

But I knew something else was missing from that. . . .

This evening Mother would be at her book club, the Red Hatted League, including half a dozen of her close gal pals who gathered regularly to discuss a mystery novel everyone was reading. Since she had been taking the same book with her, Rex Stout's *Death of a Dude*, for about six months now—which is ridiculous because it's one of the shortest

Nero Wolfe mysteries—I surmised the only discussion going on lately was of the gossiping kind.

Mother said, "I'll be at Frannie's house, dear. Don't look for me until around ten."

We were standing in the living room.

"Cora picking you up, huh?" I asked. That concerned me, as the woman was only slightly less blind than Mr. Magoo.

Mother blinked at me as if my deductive powers had suddenly improved. "Why, yes, dear—however did you know?"

"She's parked in our front lawn."

Looking out the picture window, Mother blurted, "Good Lord! Missed the driveway by a country mile. And they say *I'm* not fit to be behind the wheel!"

"Are you sure you don't want *me* to drive you?" I asked, truly concerned.

Mother shook her head. "I'll be her eyes for her, ever ready to reach over and steer."

Wasn't that reassuring?

"Okay," I said. "But keep the other hand near the door handle. Pitch and roll, and hope the new hips hold up."

"Your advice is always so helpful, dear," she said, possibly sarcastic, but maybe not.

From a table near the entryway, Mother gathered her purse and Stout book, and a plastic-wrap-covered dessert plate with her famous Heath Bar Torte, then out the door she went, for an evening with Archie, Nero, and the girls.

I watched until Cora had successfully backed out of the yard, bumping over the curb, and disappeared down the street with the horns of other cars honking fore and aft, in a friendly greeting.

After a sigh or two, I gave Sushi a treat, got my purse, and went out to the C-max, to keep my appointment with Deputy Dugan.

The address he'd given me was in Stoneybrook, an up-scale housing addition just within the city limits. Origi-nally touted as having "executive homes," Stoneybrook had been downgraded to "junior executive," as other, more expensive enclaves mushroomed near the bypass.

By any name, the homes were extremely nice, and out of many a Serenity-ite's income range, including ours. You would think that would include a deputy sheriff, whose wife didn't work, but I vaguely recalled Dugan coming from a farm family who might have had money.

Or maybe Daryl Dugan was just up to his eyeballs in debt. . . .

By dusk I was turning into the development where, off to one side, a massive rock chiseled STONEYBROOK sat like a hunkering sentinel. I crossed over a small brook, babbling (the brook, not me), and up a winding road where houses of various styles and colors were tucked back from the street among oaks, maples, and pines.

As the last rays of a pink setting sun winked through boughs, I swung into the driveway of a split-level home that sported tan siding and black shutters. I pulled up to a two-car garage whose doors were open, revealing the back ends of a silver Audi sedan and red Chevy truck.

A curved, stone-paved sidewalk took me through a well-tended lawn, then I went up a few cement steps to an etched-glass door with matching panels on either side.

I pushed the doorbell.

And waited.

Pushed again.

The door opened abruptly enough to startle me some and I was suddenly facing Daryl's wife, Candice, commonly known as Candy. A few years older than me, she had nice long blond hair, though her narrow face had a vaguely horsey cast; her best asset was a curvaceous body that she'd used to snag her various husbands (well, it sure wasn't her winning personality).

Candy was part of a large family from a blue-collar part of town that used to be known as South End. You might call it the Serenity equivalent of the wrong side of the tracks, but a girl as fetching as Candy Kowalski always had prospects.

When I was a sophomore in high school and she a senior, Candy went after a sweet, average-looking, rather immature boy in her class because—as I'd heard her say in the girls' room, one stall over—"He has a neat car and money from a part-time job." The car had been an early graduation gift from his folks, and the money he'd saved from bagging groceries was intended for college. But that summer they got married and by fall the college cash was gone, and by winter, so was Candy.

A few years later, when I was a freshman at our community college, Candy turned up on campus, taking a couple of courses, but mostly hanging out in the student lounge, trolling for another husband, soon landing one. He was a step up from the previous model, a full-time sophomore juggling a full-time job as an auto mechanic. He soon dropped out of school to provide his new wife with a better life, and after a few years, she again moved on to greener pastures.

Let me make something clear, here. I was no angel myself around this time, and probably wouldn't have married a man who was ten years older than me, and moved to Chicago, if I hadn't wanted to get away from Mother. And how did that work out?

Now Candy was Mrs. Daryl Dugan, the stay-at-home wife of a deputy likely to become sheriff, with a comfy life, and some prominence in the community. She had come a long way from South End.

Candy, wearing a tight light blue T-shirt and jeans accentuating her still-voluptuous body, said flatly, "Hello, Brandy."

"Hello, Candy," I replied not so flatly, and went in as she stepped aside.

I stood in a beige-carpeted entryway that doubled as a large landing for a half flight of stairs going up (usually in a split-level to the living room, kitchen, and bedrooms) and another half flight going down (recreation room, laundry, and spare bedroom).

Working at maintaining a strained smile, Candy was saying, "Daryl is downstairs. . . . I'll get him."

But she didn't have to, the deputy appearing at the bottom of the steps below. He also wore a tight gold Hawkeyes T-shirt and slim jeans that accentuated his buff build.

" 'lo, Brandy," Daryl said, then gestured for me to join him down there, which I did.

He led me through a recreation area where a pool table shared space with a huge flat-screen and a sectional couch, then into a smaller room that was obviously his man cave, the decor being western memorabilia. On the barn-wood walls hung spurs, bridle straps and bits, framed collections of tin stars, a smattering of signed framed photos of TV and movie star western heroes from James Arness as Matt Dillon to John Wayne as, well, John Wayne, plus reproductions of vintage wanted posters of Billy the Kid, the James Gang, and Butch Cassidy.

Another poster—this one under glass and in a fancier frame—caught my eye, and I crossed to look at the picture of a handsome mustached man with the words, *WYATT EARP FOR SHERIFF, TOMBSTONE, ARIZONA, 1881.*

Turning, I said, "I didn't know Wyatt Earp was ever sheriff of Tombstone."

I'd seen a movie or two.

Daryl, behind a small wet bar, was popping the cap on a sweating bottle of beer. "He wasn't." The deputy raised the bottle. "Want one?"

"No, thanks."

He came out from behind the bar. "Wyatt ran for sheriff but before the election took place, the gunfight at the O.K. Corral happened. Well, *near* the O.K. Corral—the name's kind of a misnomer." Daryl gestured with the bottle, smiling a proud little smile. "That's the only known circular that survived."

"You mean it's authentic?"

"You bet. There's a letter of provenance inside the back of the frame."

I took a closer look—I was antique dealer enough to be blown away. Just like the Clantons. "Wow. Where'd you get it?"

Daryl took a sip from the bottle. "An old man in town who'd collected western stuff for most of his life. Judd Pickett. Maybe you and your mother dealt with him, as dealers . . . ?"

Harriet Douglas had mentioned the Judd Pickett collection, and now the name stirred a memory from a phone conversation with Mother back when I was still living in Chicago.

"No," I said, "that was before we started actively buying and selling antiques. Wasn't he killed? In a home invasion?"

Daryl nodded. "Very sad. I was lucky, getting the poster from Judd before that happened, because his daughter wound up donating most of his collection to some museum." He cocked his head. "So, Brandy . . . what brings you to the Dugan spread?"

I took a moment to collect my thoughts. "You know, I think I'll have that beer after all."

He got back behind the bar, and I took a stool in front like a customer at the Long Branch about to unburden myself to a bartender.

Daryl handed me the cold bottle; I took a swig, then set it down. "I understand campaigns for sheriff can get pretty nasty sometimes."

Daryl grunted. "Oh, yeah. Before I came here, I ran for sheriff of a little county in Illinois, and the *lies* my opponent told about me just before the election. . . ." He shook his head. "Well, there wasn't time to refute them."

"So you know how it feels to be unfairly attacked."

The deputy gave me a hard stare. "Are you asking me to go easy on your mother? Because I'm sorry, but I won't. Really, I can't. I'm going to have to throw everything at her I can—inexperience, lack of law enforcement practice, even her run-ins with the law."

I held up a hand. "Hey, that's all fair game as far as I'm concerned. But there is one thing I'm asking you to not bring up."

"What's that?"

"Her bipolar disorder," I said, adding, "And the reason you don't have to go there is, I mean, let's face it—you're going to win, anyway."

He arched an eyebrow over one of the close-set eyes. "Vivian Borne has a *lot* of friends."

"True. And they may tell Mother they're supporting her, and maybe some of them are, but when they get into that voting booth? Almost every one of them will be marking your name."

". . . Maybe."

"Look," I said, sighing, shifting on my stool, "it's not like the whole town doesn't *already* know about her . . . eccentricities. Think how magnanimous you'll look, not bringing it up."

He thought that over.

I pressed on. "I wouldn't ask you this favor - and it *is* a favor - if I wasn't concerned that you hitting her that way—below the belt—might have bad ramifications . . . ramifications that *I'll* have to deal with. She can get thrown into a manic state or depression, and then, well, I don't even want to think about it."

He took another drink from the bottle, set it down. "Okay. I won't mention her condition." He raised a finger. "But I reserve the right to bring it up *if* I think I'm losing."

"Fair enough."

I took one last swig of my beer, then slid off the stool.

"Thanks," I said. "Oh. And, obviously, I'm hoping we can keep this conversation between us. Mother would be very hurt if she knew."

"Sure," Daryl said, smiling and shrugging. "And I'll tell Candy we talked about campaign procedure. Just kind of established some parameters."

"And that's not a lie, either, is it?"

Another smile. "No."

A few minutes later I was about to get into my car, when a hand landed on my shoulder and spun me around.

"Just why are you *here*?" Candy demanded.

"Hey!"

"Is it something *Harriet* told you?" she asked.

"What? No. Campaign procedure. Mother's never done this before. I'm her campaign manager—I thought Daryl and I should establish some ground rules."

Candy pointed a red-nailed finger in my face. "You'd better not *ruin* this for me!"

And she marched back toward the house, leaving me standing in the driveway, wondering what *that* was all about. . . .

A *Trash 'n' Treasures Tip*

Sometimes white elephant sales have a "preview night" where buyers—for an added price—can have a chance to buy before the general public does. Mother splits the cost with a friend . . . then attends for both of them, cell phone at the ready.

Chapter Four

The Sick and the Dead

D earest ones!
Vivian here, taking the narrative ball from Brandy, which I know will please many of you in the "Viva Vivian!" crowd. But before I continue with our exciting tale, I simply must get a few things off my bosom. (I know the term is "chest," but that has such a harsh sound, don't you think?)

The other day I was having lunch at a local eatery, noted for their exceptional haddock plate (best sampled early in the week). Anyhoo, while I sat ruminating (wonderful word!) over my after-meal coffee, a young waitress stopped by and refilled my cup. I responded with the appropriate, "Thank you," and she replied, "No problem."

So I asked her, "Oh, *was* there a problem?"

And she replied, "Huh?"

Then I said, "Because I thought keeping my cup filled was part of your job, not a favor you were doing me." Well, she gave me a dirty look and left (and didn't refill my cup again). I'm afraid this latest generation has lost all sense of polite behavior.

Since when did *no problem* become interchangeable

with *you're welcome*? It's not as though saying the former saves any more time or effort than the latter. And the phrase *no problem* consists of two negative words. Talk about sending out bad vibes!

Replying "no problem" is appropriate only after someone asks someone else to do them a favor, the response indicating the askee is receptive to the idea, as when I was caught downtown without wheels and needed to get promptly elsewhere, and flagged down a young man on a motorcycle. When I explained my dilemma (I may have exaggerated just a teensy bit by saying it was a life or death matter), he replied, "No problem." *Correct-oh-mundo!* So I hopped on the back of the Harley, glad I was wearing slacks, and off we went, the wind having its way with my hair.

So I'm asking you, dear reader, to join me in reversing this abomination of misusage by pointing it out (politely, of course) (assuming you want more coffee) whenever you encounter the unfortunate response, "no problem." Together we can change the world, one waitress at a time!

You're welcome!

While I'm on the subject of restaurants, something else I've regularly been subjected to has been gnawing at me like a miffed Sushi with one of Brandy's shoes, specifically the overuse of the word *awesome*, often uttered by waitstaff after my positive response to a meal. How can my pleasure in a meal possibly be awesome? Worse yet, sometimes my very *order* has been deemed worthy of such a superlative!

Awesome is used nowadays for the most mundane things, which emasculates the term. Among "awesome" occurrences would be a shooting star, a dog that could talk, or my bunions not hurting after a long walk. So let's put the *awe* back in *awesome*!

(**Note to Vivian from Editor:** *Would you please move the narrative along?*)

(**Note to Editor from Vivian:** *Yes, ma'am.*)
(**Note to Vivian from Editor:** *Awesome.*)
(**Note to Editor from Vivian:** *No problem!*)

The Red Hatted League was formed by myself and a few close friends who had become disenchanted by our experience in the Red Hat Society, an organization of ladies aged fifty or older (I just barely made the age requirement!) who meet regularly for lunch wearing red hats and purple dresses, and whose mantra is *just having fun.*

Well, our RHS group was having a little too much fun, accused as we were of intemperate imbibing (is that redundant?) during dinner, leading to more than a few fender-benders in restaurant parking lots. I do not drink myself—doing so interferes with my medication (once I partook of spirits and ended up in Poughkeepsie, remembering neither how I'd gone or why) (well, by bus), nor did I find flattering festooning myself in red or purple (just *try* to find a purple dress!). So I approached a few like-minded members to spin off the main group, like *Rhoda* from *The Mary Tyler Moore Show*, and join me instead in a mystery readers' book club.

Granted, our little group of five didn't seem to be critiquing many books of late, having a much better time gathering at our homes (instead of a noisy restaurant) to share Serenity intel, and enjoy each other's company whilst partaking of wonderful homemade desserts.

We meet twice a month because once a month is not enough time to catch up on all the news (*Brandy aside:* gossip), and once a week did not provide enough newsworthy material to justify an every-seven-days assault on our various waistlines, due to too many fattening desserts. This is not to say that we don't ever discuss a mystery novel—our average is a respectable two per annum.

This evening Frannie Phillips was hostess, and I was the Bestower of Dessert (a floating officer position), as we didn't feel it fair that the hostess should have to straighten her house *and* bake something. (When I was hosting, I only cleaned the room we'd be in, and the downstairs bath. Climb the stairs, you take your chances!)

By some miracle, Cora and I arrived at Frannie's in one piece, the woman even managing to parallel park her Buick without hitting those fore and aft, although her car took root about a foot and a half from the curb, and when we exited the vehicle, I had to grab Cora's arm to keep her from getting out in front of a swerving pickup truck.

Cora was petite, with bird-like head movements reminiscent of the English stage and screen actress Elsa Lanchester in *Bride of Frankenstein*, although Cora didn't have a British accent or for that matter white streaks at her dark temples (actually, Cora had dark streaks at her white temples). At one time she (Cora not Elsa) had been a courtroom secretary, and knew all the lawyers in town and their business, which had encouraged me to get to know her. I do need my sources!

Frannie met us at the door of her one-story redbrick bungalow. With her long face, pointed chin, and wiry gray hair, she reminded me of Margaret Hamilton, *The Wizard of Oz*'s Wicked Witch of the West, sans green face, of course. Frannie was a retired nurse, knowledgeable about many things medical, which, at our age, made her handy to have around.

Cora and I stepped inside.

Since Frannie had retired from the hospital, she'd become a much-improved housekeeper. Back when she was working, and wives were still expected to do all the housework and cooking, Frannie used a trick that I thought was brilliant.

Just before her husband was due home from the office, she'd set out all of her cleaning supplies, tie a bandana around her hair, and drag the vacuum out in the middle of the floor. Then, when he pulled his car into the drive, she'd get busy. Hubby would come in, see her working hard, feel her pain, and offer to take her out for dinner. I bet Frannie only cooked once or twice a week back then!

The other two members of our club, Alice Hetzler and Norma Crumley, had already arrived and were seated on the floral couch in the living room, their Rex Stout books in their laps.

Alice was tall and thin, plain and proper, recalling Jane Hathaway of *The Beverly Hillbillies*. A former middle school English teacher, Alice had an opinion on everything, and in my opinion, was batting about .300.

(In response to a rare critical review of a prior book, I must state that, no, not everyone in Serenity resembles a TV or movie star. A surprising number do, however, and anyway, as an actress myself, I tend to think in showbiz terms. Can anyone claim that these little comparisons don't help a reader "cast" the characters herein? I rest my case, as Raymond Burr used to say. Loved that man—wish an eligible bachelor around town looked like *him*!)

(**Note to Vivian from Editor:** *Mrs. Borne . . . get a handle on these digressions. . . .*)

(**Note to Editor from Vivian:** *Yes, ma'am. But you sound just like Sergeant Carter on* Gomer Pyle*!*)

Norma was a newbie to our group, and at fifty-five the youngest (I always leave myself out of these calculations). She was zaftig (isn't that a lovely word?) and kept her short hair dyed black, though frankly wore a smidgen more makeup than need be, and quite overdid the jewelry. If I took off my glasses and squinted, she looked like Elizabeth Taylor during her Michael Jackson/Studio 54 days.

As a human, Norma was an acquired taste, considered by many pushy and loud, but a prominent socialite in the community before her banker husband found a younger wife, leaving Norma alone to bask in her settlement. But once he dumped her, so did most of her friends, because those "friends" apparently had only put up with Norma because of him.

We didn't mind spending time with her (in small doses), because she was still the best conveyer of news in town, gathering all kinds of interesting tidbits from her cleaning lady, hairdresser, manicurist, and stylist, conduits to which the rest of us lacked regular access.

Frannie relieved me of my plastic-wrap-covered dessert plate, conveying it to the kitchen, and I moved to a straight-back chair opposite Norma and Alice on the couch. Cora settled into an overstuffed easy chair next to me, her feet barely touching the carpet, like a first grader at a fifth grader's desk. Our hostess returned and took the only spot left, a recliner next to the sofa.

I should mention one other member who inevitably joined us at Frannie's—Miss Lizzie, a bearded dragon lizard. Brown and yellow, about a foot long, she usually stayed in her aquarium in the corner, but Lizzie rather seemed to enjoy our company and, once Frannie took a seat, Miss Lizzie would climb out of the glass box, slither over and up Frannie's chair to perch on her mistress's shoulder.

Oddly, the reptile seemed to listen to our discourse, wearing a perpetual smile, alert eyes moving from speaker to speaker. Now and then its (her?) mouth would open as if Miss Lizzie had something to add to the conversation, but couldn't find the words, flicking a tongue to lick the air, and shutting its fly trap yet again.

Still, I preferred Frannie's grinning lizard over Alice's squawking parrot—the ex-English teacher having no more luck teaching it to speak properly than she'd had with decades of students—or Cora's nervous, never-housebroken Chihuahua, or Norma's fat, ever-eating, ever-being-fed tabby. These pets were part of the proceedings only in the individual homes of their mistresses. Of course, all the girls loved Sushi when they came to our house.

Opening my book, *Death of a Dude*, I said, "I believe we left off in chapter three, just before Nero arrives at the dude ranch." It was a rarity when the corpulent, rather lazy sleuth left his brownstone.

Our hostess said, "Don't get me wrong, Vivian, but could we do an author other than Rex Stout if we ever finish this one? You've insisted on Nero and Archie ever since we formed the club."

"Possibly, at some point." I had not revealed to the girls that I intended the league to keep reading Stout until Brandy and I won a Nero Award (we were nominated twice!). "So Nero Wolfe is just about to arrive. . . ."

"No," said Alice, "he's already at the ranch—we're in chapter four. I remember because a taxi brought his luggage separately."

"You're both wrong," countered Frannie. "We're in chapter five, where Archie and Nero go for a hike so they won't be overheard, and Nero takes a tumble down a hill."

"He *almost* fell down the hill," Cora corrected.

"Poor Harriet," Norma remarked.

We stared at her. I didn't recall a Harriet in the book.

"Harriet *Douglas*!" Norma scolded, in a how-soon-they-forget tone.

"Oh!" we all said, followed by assorted appropriate adjectives—*terrible, horrible, unfortunate,* etc.

Miss Lizzie's smile, however, was inappropriate.

"Viv," Alice said, voice dripping with concern, "I heard you were there with Brandy just before the explosion, and that your daughter actually got *hurt*."

"Brandy's fine," I said with finality, not wanting to waste time on the girl's minor injuries.

"Tell us what happened," Norma said eagerly.

"Yes, do!" the others chimed in.

So I did, beginning with our visit to Harriet's apartment, and ending with the big bang.

When I'd completed my discourse, Frannie said, "I *warned* Harriet not to smoke around that oxygen tank."

"You've seen her do that?" I asked. Frannie regularly volunteered her nursing skills at Sunny Meadow and would be in a position to know.

"I never actually *saw* her do it," Frannie replied, "but her apartment smelled like the aftermath of a *bonfire* whenever I'd go in."

"Well, I *did* see her do that," Cora commented. "I paid her a visit not long ago, and there she was, puffing away next to that oxygen tank. I said, 'Harriet—smoke outside and away from that tank!' And she just shrugged and said, 'Usually I do . . . but it's *raining.*'"

Hadn't it just started to rain, when Brandy went back to give Harriet our book?

Norma was saying, "I'm not surprised something like that happened at Sunny Meadow, considering all the violations imposed since that Burnett character took over as manager."

My tongue flicked out like Miss Lizzie's. "Violations?" I asked.

Norma looked aghast. "Vivian, where have *you* been? You're usually on top of all the local tittle-tattle."

I was feigning ignorance, a tactic I fall back on frequently. I *had* heard the tittle-tattle about violations, but didn't mind letting Norma feel superior, if it meant getting information I might not have.

Cora piled on. "Why, there was a two-part front-page article about the trouble at Sunny Meadow in the *Serenity Sentinel*. Didn't you read it, Vivian?"

I had not. I'd dropped the newspaper some time ago, in

retaliation for a lackluster review of my one-woman per-
formance of Libby Wolfson's masterpiece, "I'm Taking
My Own Head, Screwing It On Right, and No Guy's
Gonna Tell Me That It Ain't."

"What did the article say?" I asked.

Cora deferred to Norma, who settled deeper in the couch.
"Well, since Mr. Burnett took over out there, Sunny Meadow
has been fined for"—the socialite started counting on fingers
loaded with expensive rings—"having insufficient nursing
staff, accidents due to inadequate supervision, nonfunc-
tioning security cameras, errors in dispensing medications,
not maintaining the patient's personal hygiene—"

Alice interrupted: "Louise Rockwell told me she had a
bed sore that got so bad they nearly amputated her leg!"

"That would have put a crimp in her ballroom dancing," I said sympathetically. Louise and her late husband
had made *Dancing with the Stars* look ridiculous.

Leaning forward, more bird-like than ever, missing only
a branch, Cora said, "And I heard from Arthur Fillmore
that Burnett had such trouble getting help, what with the
low wages he paid, that he's taken to hiring ex-convicts."

Miss Lizzie opened her mouth as if to add her two cents,
but closed it again, keeping her (its?) opinion to itself (herself?).

I said, "Well, having made the acquaintance of a convict
or two, in my travels and travails, I find it admirable, em-
ploying those who've served their penance to society."

"Maybe so," Norma said, "but when I went to see
Goldie Goldstein, just after she took that terrible fall last
year? She said the pain pills she was given didn't work at
all. I mean, pain pills should *work*, shouldn't they?"

Frannie had been quiet throughout this exchange, but
now the retired nurse, and volunteer at the facility, spoke.
"Girls, I don't think you realize how difficult it is to run a
nursing home. The majority of patients are on Medicaid,

and the government can be slow in paying and creditors don't always understand that. I'm sure Mr. Burnett works hard to keep Sunny Meadow afloat, grappling with ever-increasing costs, while trying to comply with a growing list of both state and federal regulations."

Considering the number of violations that had already been imposed, I wondered if Burnett thought paying fines was more cost effective than implementing expensive recommendations. But I reserved that thought for myself.

Frannie went on, "Furthermore, I don't think it's helpful to spread rumors about nearly amputated legs, or pills that don't seem to work, or ex-convicts possibly hired as help . . . rumors that are, in my opinion, either exaggerated or unsubstantiated."

Her feathers had been ruffled, so I tried to smooth them.

"You're right, of course, dear. Assisted-living facilities are only going to become more and more important to society as the Baby Boom generation ages, particularly as a cure for Alzheimer's disease remains out of reach, what with the general population living longer and longer. We can all take a page out of Frannie's playbook by volunteering at such facilities."

Except for me, because I had essentially been banned from the local facilities, my volunteer work mistaken for "snooping." Can you imagine? No good deed!

I continued, "Even a few hours a week would bring smiles to lonely faces and give the overworked staff a little support."

There, that should do the trick where unruffling our hostess was concerned.

The others murmured their agreement.

"Thank you, Vivian," Frannie said. Then the woman dropped a real bombshell. "What *does* concern me is the unusually high death rate this year at Sunny Meadow."

No one spoke for a moment. But my antennae were tingling.

I asked, "There's, uh, nothing *untoward* about those deaths, perchance?"

Frannie looked startled, though some of that may have been due to my invoking the little-used but effective *perchance*.

"Oh, goodness, no!" she said. "I wasn't implying anything *sinister*. Nor that these unfortunate deaths had to do with the quality of care out there. Not at all! I only wish to see the patients thrive and survive as long as they can."

"Dear," Alice said softly, "many of those patients want to be released from this life. The ones I visit, anyway."

"Sunny Meadow is a *nursing home*," Cora said. "Dying is what people do there."

The former court secretary could be rather tactless, and the comment raised Frannie's hackles once again.

Our hostess gestured with a dismissive hand, Miss Lizzie bouncing on her owner's shoulder. "Look, just forget I said *anything*!"

But that was not going to happen—not with me in the room, anyway. I'd already filed everything away in the Vivian Borne memory bank.

"Why don't we have dessert," I said cheerfully. "I could use a sugar boost!"

Which wasn't precisely true. A recent blood test revealed my glucose level at prediabetic levels. Middle of the night scoops of chocolate-chip mint ice cream had finally taken their toll. So had the Toll House cookies.

"And then we'll drop all this talk of death," I said, "and get back to murder."

"Good idea," replied Frannie, smiling now, Miss Lizzie, too. She removed the reptile from her shoulder, returned it to the glass house, then she and I went into her kitchen to prepare the refreshments. Soon we were all enjoying de-caffeinated coffee along with my delicious concoction. (I had a tiny piece.)

Heath Bar Torte

3 egg whites
¾ cups and 2 tbl. sugar
½ tsp. vanilla
½ pint whipped cream
6 Heath bars, or ½ lb. of chocolate-covered toffee pieces,
   broken into small bits.

In a chilled bowl, add the vanilla to the egg whites and beat, gradually adding in the sugar, and continue beating until stiff peaks form. Spread the meringue in a 1-inch-thick circle on parchment paper on cookie sheet. Bake at 275 one hour, until set and lightly browned. Turn off the oven and leave inside 2 hours. Remove meringue and cut in half. Whip the cream, and fold in the broken candy. Transfer bottom half of the meringue to a pretty plate or dish and spread with half of the whipped cream/candy frosting; repeat layers, covering torte completely with frosting. Refrigerate.

Yield: 8 servings.

When we had finished eating—Norma, Alice, and Cora partaking of seconds—the conversation soon drifted from Rex Stout to grandchildren and general ailments, and I signaled to Cora that it was time to depart. She nodded in discreet agreement.

I retrieved my empty serving plate from the kitchen, thanked our hostess, bid good-bye to the others, then Cora and I took our leave.

We hadn't traveled very far in the Buick when she said, "There are a lot of people at Sunny Meadow who are not unhappy about Harriet's departure."

"Staff, you mean?" I asked.

She nodded, keeping her eyes uselessly on the road. "And others."

Usually, I try to limit our conversation, in hopes Cora might not wrap the car around a telephone pole. But this line of talk seemed worth the risk.

"*What* others?" I pressed.

"All I know is that Harriet made trouble for anybody who she thought was breaking the rules—staff *or* residents."

And yet, Harriet broke rules herself, smoking in her room near that oxygen tank.

Cora was saying, "Don't get me wrong—most of the residents loved her for advocating for them, standing up for them, even going so far as to give testimony about violations that led to fines."

"But she was not, I assumed, beloved by the staff."

She nodded again, as a car honked at her for hogging the center line. "Especially Mr. Burnett. He wanted to expel Harriet from the facility for smoking inside her apartment, but could never catch her red-handed."

"Who else on the staff might have wished her ill?"

Cora shrugged. "Any one of the ones she'd had a run-in with."

Alas, the conversation ended as we had arrived at my abode, Cora missing the driveway again, this time guiding the Buick over a bed of my prized petunias. But then flowers are always doomed to a short life. And, anyway, my bunions were grateful for getting me close to the front door.

I thanked her for the lift—"Always exciting, dear!"— and exited the car.

Inside, Sushi greeted me with love and enthusiasm until she realized the platter in my hand was empty. So off she trotted. Where did she learn such selfish behavior?

I found Brandy in the dining room seated at the Duncan Phyfe table; she was in her jammies, having hot chocolate topped with tiny marshmallows.

She gestured to her cup. "I'm having this because I figured there wouldn't be any torte left."

"Good call, dear," I said, setting the empty dish on the table. "How was *your* evening?"

"Okay . . . and yours?"

I pulled out a chair and sat down. "Most interesting."

"Oh?"

I told her Cora had actually seen Harriet smoking around her oxygen tank.

Brandy nodded. "That's what we figured caused the explosion. Hope you're not disappointed it's not murder. What else did your friends have to say?"

Since she seemed genuinely interested—which isn't always the case—I told her about the nursing home violations, and the various allegations made by the girls.

"So maybe," I said, "murder isn't off the table, after all."

After a moment, Brandy said, "Sunny Meadow isn't the only nursing home to have violations, you know—it's not really all that uncommon. And so what if Mr. Burnett hired ex-convicts? They've served their time, and need jobs."

"I quite agree."

"Just as long as they perform the jobs sufficiently." She paused. "And, regarding pain pills . . . they don't always work the same way for everyone."

"Granted," I said. "Then what about the high rate of deaths that Frannie alluded to?"

She shrugged. "People who have long-term care insurance are staying in their homes until the policies run out.

So they're arriving at nursing homes in worse shape than before—checking in when it's about time to check out."

I pursed my lips. "I hardly expected you to take Sunny Meadow's side, after you were nearly blown to bits due to their negligence."

"I'm not sure they were negligent, Mother. If Harriet ignored the restriction of not smoking around an oxygen tank, isn't it *her* fault that something happened?"

The girl was really getting my dander up.

I huffed, "Well, *I* am not at all convinced the explosion was an accident."

Her eyes narrowed. "Why not?"

"Because Harriet was a troublemaker at Sunny Meadow, a sort of whistle-blower, who made scads of enemies."

Brandy sighed. "No one killed Harriet, Mother. She did that to herself." She cocked her head. "Why do I think you're just looking for another crime to solve?"

"Don't be ridiculous. Why ever would I do that?"

"Normally I'd say, for the fun of it. But maybe you think nabbing another murderer would help put you in office. Think again—running for sheriff is a full-time job. You don't have time for another case, even if this *is* one— which it isn't."

I said nothing.

"Besides," she went on, "you can't go snooping around Sunny Meadow. You're persona non grata out there. What legitimate excuse could you come up with, for being out at that place?"

Again I said nothing. It does happen occasionally.

Brandy pushed back her chair and stood. "The only way you could really investigate your suspicion that Harriet was done in was if you were *staying* out at Sunny Meadow, and you're too young for that . . . remember?"

"You're right on that account, dear," I said, nodding.

Brandy picked up her cup. "Good. Then you'll forget about Harriet and focus on the campaign."

"No," I replied, "I won't be able to. But we can confer out at Sunny Meadow, where I'll be recuperating."

"Recuperating? Recuperating from what?"

"My podiatrist says it's about time I had these bothersome bunions operated on, and I know Sunny Meadow is the perfect place to heal up."

The cup fell from Brandy's hand and shattered on the floor. Preferable to a spit take, I'd say.

Mother's Trash 'n' Treasures Tip

To get the best selection at a white elephant sale, go early, but anticipate a long queue. To get the best price, go later, but expect less selection. To get the best parking place, leave your car the night before and have someone drop you off at the door, just before the sale opens.

Chapter Five

Have Wheels—Will Travel

This is Vivian once again, coming to you from my new digs at Sunny Meadow Manor, second floor, room 205, which had recently been vacated by another temp patient who had gone home after convalescing from a double hip replacement. (Been there, done that.)

Merely a week has passed since I made the decision to have the bunions on my feet operated upon (I'm not sure bunions turn up anywhere else *but* feet), and as luck would have it, when I called my podiatrist to set up the surgery, he'd just had a cancellation from Mrs. Beatrice Fromer and I could take her slot two days hence.

Well, in case she knew something I didn't, I gave Beatrice a call to find out exactly why she had gotten cold feet—I'll pause while you chuckle—and she informed me the cancellation had nada to do with concern over the operation itself, nor skill of the surgeon, but everything to do with the *Lady Luck* riverboat casino!

Apparently, the woman simply loved to gamble on the aforementioned paddlewheel, which traversed the Mississippi from Dubuque to Fort Madison and back again, docking in river towns such as ours along the way, taking on passengers going nowhere, though often a good deal of their money was from making a one-way trip.

Anticipating being laid up for many weeks, and unable to navigate her two too-sore feet to her beloved one-armed bandits, Beatrice made multiple presurgery trips onboard, where each time her aching bunions "spoke to her" and led her to a winning slot. How could she pass up such inside info, giving her a rare advantage over the house (houseboat)?

My bunions spoke to me, as well, but limited their precognition to the weather, specifically impending rain. But I could get those particulars from the weather channel, without the suffering. So I was fine in saying adieu to the gruesome twosome.

There are three different procedures to correct protruding bunions: an osteotomy, which involves making a cut along the side of the big toe, then realigning the bunion to its normal position; an exostectomy, the removal of the bunion from the joint without an alignment; and an arthrodesis, where the surgeon replaces the damaged joint with screws or metal plates to correct the deformity. (*Warning:* refrain from Googling images of any of these procedures before eating. And if you choose the latter procedure, prepare in future to set off airport security alarms.)

Fortunately, the procedure I selected was an osteotomy, the least extreme. Nonetheless, it required casts on both feet, though to be soon replaced by medical boots, and—with the assistance of crutches—I should be able to walk a little, at which time, according to the terms of my insurance, I'll get thrown out of here like a sot from a saloon.

So I had much to accomplish in a limited time frame.

As you may recall, Sunny Meadow Manor was a large, two-story, redbrick facility, with the assisted-living apartments, reception area, and staff offices on the first floor.

The second floor comprised everything else: nursing home patients, Alzheimer's wing, cafeteria, library, chapel, music/entertainment area, and several other rooms for private family gatherings. There was even a little coffee shop.

My quarters were small (though admittedly larger than the cells I've inhabited at the county jail) with a hospital-type bed, nightstand, three-drawer dresser, recliner, TV, closet, and bathroom with shower. Brandy had thoughtfully contributed a few welcoming items from home, like the Victorian crazy quilt I'd saved from a dumpster (which admittedly had a few holes in it) (the blanket, not the dumpster), and several of my best nightgowns as well as a comfy robe.

The dear girl had also gathered some track suits with zippers up the legs to accommodate the casts, so I didn't have to spend my stay in pj's. Additionally, I had my cell phone and charger, address book, Mary Kay beauty products, and AARP magazines with helpful articles, although I'm not really big on taking advice—I've lived this long doing things the Vivian Borne way! So I just admired the pictures of how well-preserved Warren Beatty, Diane Keaton, and Helen Mirren appear. There's hope for us all! Hope, and Photoshop.

Brandy also brought my framed picture of Gabby Hayes to keep me company, which I positioned facing me on my bedside table—although I suspect the child just wanted him off the mantel and out of the house. Gabby's smiling if toothless face at my bedside did get a few strange looks from the Manor staff, but jealousy is one disease even the best health care can't cure. Plus, there was a fresh vase of spring flowers sunning itself on my wide windowsill, compliments of the Red Hatted League girls.

So I was snug as a bug in a rug! A bug whose bunions had been realigned, that is, although considering how many legs and little feet some bugs have, maybe a new cliché is in order.

This is not to say there weren't a few adjustments to be made by the Sunny Meadow Manor staff, starting with a little dustup with top dog George Burnett. It had to do with insurance and policy, specifically my insistence on using a special kind of wheelchair, one of which they had in storage, lighter weight than the usual ones, with bigger wheels with hand-rims, and lacking the back handlebars for someone to push me.

These wheelchair accessories would enable me to get around faster by myself. The end result of the negotiation had me signing a waiver releasing the facility from culpability in the unlikely possibility that anything might go awry.

There was also a minor kerfuffle with registered nurse Joan Lindle, a female scarecrow in her midforties, who howled at me like a harpy after I left my room without informing her. But this was settled by Brandy sticking a writing board on my door—like college students have in their dorms?—upon which I would record my whereabouts. The actual accuracy of the whereabouts I listed was for me to know and the nurse to find out.

Now that I was settled in, I began my investigation in earnest. For while my bunions indeed had been due for a tune-up, I was using that excuse to give me good and thorough access to Sunny Meadow and its denizens.

As the spring morning outside found the sun shining itself silly, I waited till after breakfast, which I skipped—why wake the beast before lunch?—to wheel myself to the central elevator and descend to the first floor's assisted-living apartments. My mode of transport (the wheelchair, not the elevator) was light and swift, and almost better than legs and feet, particularly when the latter weren't bunion-free.

I was wearing one of the zipper-leg track suits in periwinkle blue—not according to my color chart, I admit, but I hadn't mentioned that to Brandy, not wanting to appear ungrateful. I rolled myself off the elevator, then along the hallway, my destination the quarters of Mrs. Goldie Goldstein, who had donated the Louis Vuitton suitcase to my cause.

Passing by poor Harriet's former apartment, I noted that repairs had been made: new door, repainted outside walls, even new carpeting in that area—fast, efficient work, for a facility so often criticized. It was almost as if the explosion had never happened, but for a faint, scorched aroma still lingering in the air, like our kitchen after Brandy ruined something.

The next apartment was Goldie's, and I leaned forward in my wheelchair and knocked on the door, which opened after a few moments.

"Vivian," the woman said, smiling pleasantly. "I heard through the grapevine that you were sailing the Good Ship Sunny Meadow."

I always wonder if I should correct that kind of thing—what sort of ship has a grapevine on it? But a professional writer like myself mustn't expect precision from amateurs.

As always, Goldie was impeccably dressed, having owned a local women's clothing store for years—I took perverse pleasure in trading there, where no prices were on the tags and you were required to bargain as if at an Arabian bazaar. Today's pleasantly plump hostess was attired in a navy jacket over cream-colored silk blouse with a bow at the neck, tailored tan slacks, and brown leather loafers with tassels. Her short silver hair was styled attractively, and she wore just the right amount of rouge.

"Up for a visit?" I asked.

"I'd love a chat," she replied, beaming down at me.

Her positive response was a relief, because I was already

wheeling forward, and might have rolled over her expensive shoes had she not stepped aside.

Goldie's apartment was furnished in the Chippendale style, of which I am not a fan. Following as it did the simple elegance of the Queen Anne period that I preferred, Chippendale tried too hard with its overly ornate wood carvings, taloned (claw-and-ball) feet, and dependency on pointed pediments and finials.

I wheeled forward into the compact living room area, and parked in the only spot large enough to accommodate my vehicle, which was in front of the coffee table and next to a particularly unattractive, excessively carved chair, with large lion-paw feet. Ugh—who wants their furniture to appear about to pounce? But to each her own.

"How are you, Vivian dear?" Goldie asked, adding, "If there's anything I can do to help you while you're here, please let me know."

"Just need a little time being pampered," I said, "while the toot-toot-tootsies are on the mend."

She nodded, still smiling, as she slid into the ugly chair.

"You needn't worry about me," I said. "I already know my way around this place, although I grant you, it's different from the perspective of a patient."

She nodded. "Moving here took a little adjustment on my part, as well. It's the same for everyone."

I cocked my head. "You seem much too fit for assisted living, dear. Why didn't you stay in your lovely home?"

I already knew, of course. Goldie had no family or relatives in town anymore, her daughter (a lawyer) on the West Coast, her son (a doctor) on the East Coast. After she'd taken several tumbles at home, they insisted she live with one of them. When Goldie refused to relocate and leave her many friends, a compromise was made for her to move to Sunny Meadow.

So I politely listened to her story, inserting appropriate

nods and nonverbal responses and prompts. I had hoped she might volunteer some dirt about her stay thus far at the facility, but learned nothing new for my trouble. But it was a good way to grease the wheels (not my wheelchair's—the metaphorical ones).

When Goldie had finished, I said, "Well, I for one am glad you're here—you certainly add class to this facility!"

I make it a policy to compliment someone I'm about to interrogate—I mean, *interview*—to put them further at ease.

Goldie smiled. "How sweet of you to say so." Her eyes traveled to my casts. "Do tell me about your operation."

Since this was not what I wanted to spend time discussing—past a certain age, people seem to want to endlessly recount their own operations, though their eyes glaze when the operations of their peers are detailed—I asked, "What is that *marvelous* smell emanating from the kitchen?"

Her eyes glittered. "Chocolate babka! Have you had breakfast?"

I admitted I hadn't, despite the Sunny Meadow dietician lecturing me that breakfast was the most important meal of the day.

"You *must* have some, then," she said. "Breakfast is the most important meal of the day, you know."

It is when it's fresh homemade chocolate babka!

When I demurred (not too convincingly), saying I didn't want to put her to any trouble, she responded, "Nonsense. And I'll join you. Coffee or tea?"

Soon we were enjoying the most scrumptious coffee cake known to God or man, and sipping hot tea from delicate china cups.

Goldie patted her lips with a white linen napkin. "You were going to tell me about your operation."

I not so elegantly wiped my mouth. "Would you mind if

we save that for another time? The details are nothing to share over babka."

She raised her eyebrows. "I had no idea. . . ."

"Yes, well, if you ever go that route, have the surgeon put you under. You don't want to be awake, even though you can't feel a thing."

"Oh, my."

That shut the topic down. And kept the babka down, too.

I shifted in my wheelchair, which for all its merits could have used more padding. "Now, about Harriet . . . did you ever see her smoking around her oxygen tank?"

Goldie shook her head. "As far as I know, she went outside on her patio without the tank, even in winter." She gestured toward the kitchen. "I could see her from my window over the sink . . . but every now and then—not too often—when I walked past her door? I could strongly smell cigarette smoke, which gave me the impression she sometimes cheated."

"When it was raining, perhaps?"

My hostess frowned in thought. "Now that you mention it, yes. There's no protection over these patios when it rains."

I switched gears (metaphorically—my chair had no gears, and anyway I wasn't moving). "I understand when you came here after that last bad spill of yours, you were on the second floor for a while."

She nodded. "I needed better care—couldn't just be alone in one of these apartments."

"You were on a pain medication at that time?"

". . . Yes."

"Which didn't help?"

She frowned. "Who told you that? However could you know?"

"Just a wild guess."

"A wild guess named Norma Crumley?"

When I didn't answer, Goldie smirked. "Vivian, you'd be wise to be careful what you say around that woman."

No worries there—I was a sponge, not a spigot. (Another metaphor—isn't colorful language fun?)

"Is it true?" I asked. "About the pills not being effective, I mean." (I already knew the truth about Norma Crumley spreading tales.)

She nodded. "Funny thing—I'd been on that same medication before, and it worked wonderfully well. But not *this* time."

"What do you make of that?"

Goldie leaned forward, placed her plate on the coffee table, and leaned back. "I don't know that I should say."

"I'm not *Norma*, dear."

She studied me a moment. "Well, of course I knew that a medication that worked in one instance might not work in another—though both times I'd had a fall. But I suspected . . ."

"Suspected what, dear?"

My hostess sighed. "I thought an over-the-counter pain medication might have been substituted."

"Something cheap and less effective."

She nodded. "Something cheap, less effective."

Wanda Mercer was an LPN who distributed the patient's daily doses; but Joan Lindle, an RN, was in charge of ordering the medications and keeping track of them.

Goldie was saying, "Whether the nursing home was trying to save money with some inferior brand, or someone was pilfering, I couldn't say."

"Did you share these thoughts with Harriet, perchance?"

"Yes. She looked out for us, all of us girls out here . . . so she'd want to know."

I smiled. "From what I'm hearing, Harriet was pretty popular among the residents."

Goldie chuckled. "And pretty *unpopular* with the staff."

"Anyone in particular?"

The woman lowered her voice. "Who do you think? Mr. Burnett. I heard him arguing with her the morning she died—right through my bedroom wall! Her living room was just on the other side."

I sat forward. "When was this, dear?"

She pondered that for a moment. "Between nine and nine-thirty that morning . . . well before you and Brandy stopped by."

"Could you hear what was being said?"

She shook her head. "Too muffled. But it was an argument, all right. And Burnett did most of the shouting."

He would.

I thanked Goldie for the visit, and when she offered me a piece of babka to take along, I accepted, not wanting to hurt her feelings, of course. My wheelchair had a little saddlebag where I could temporarily store the yummy snack, though if I didn't watch my sugar intake, I'd be back at somewhere like this on a more permanent basis.

My next stop was farther down the hall to the apartment of Louise Rockwell, who had donated the starburst clock to my white elephant sale, and I was wheeling along briskly when I encountered Wanda.

"Oh, there you are!" the young nurse said, coming toward me pushing a dispensary cart on wheels.

Wanda was a shade on the heavy side—with a pretty, round face, short dark hair, and invisible wire-frame glasses—and wore a floral smock, white slacks, and clog-like shoes.

"Mrs. Borne," she sighed, "I do wish you'd stay in your room until I've given you your morning medication."

"I'll try to postpone my wanderings in future, dear. What medicinal delights have you for me?"

She consulted a chart. "An antibiotic and pain pill."

"Very well. Have you some water?"

She did. I was about to pop the two pills into my mouth when I stopped.

"No pain pill this morning," I said, eyeing the opioid. "I don't believe I need one . . . and besides, it disrupts my, uh, plumbing, if you know what I mean."

Wanda withdrew the pill. "All right. Will you want one tonight?"

"Well, dear, we'll know the answer to that when evening arrives, won't we?"

She gave me a smirk and a grunt—not long on repartee, this girl—and rumbled on with the cart.

I might come to regret not taking that pill (unless an over-the-counter softball had been substituted for a hard-core opioid), as my feet *were* giving me some trouble; but it was more important for me to put bait in the trap. I knew that every pill had to be accounted for, whether the patient took it or not.

Arriving at Louise's apartment, I found her presence there no surprise—I'd learned she rarely took advantage of the morning activities offered, such as exercise classes, sing-alongs, and crafts.

Louise was a stooped (though not stupid) woman, with permed gray hair, glasses thicker than mine, and a fondness for wearing old-fashioned cotton housedresses like those found in the Vermont Country Store catalogue (which regularly came to my house because I'd once ordered some foot-soaking crystals). Today's dress might have been sewn from a red-checkered tablecloth.

We sat in a living room with mismatched inexpensive furniture, from home, no doubt—era-mixing like that reflected the passage of time, or a trip to the thrift shop. Louise was sitting back in a recliner, with me parked next to her on a couch whose springs sprang eternal. I was offered no refreshment.

"I'd like to thank you," I said graciously, "for the lovely clock you gave me."

"I did?"

Louise was at Sunny Meadow because of her faulty memory. Word on the street (actually the social areas) was, she might be moved upstairs to the Alzheimer's Unit if she wandered off the grounds one more time.

"Yes," I said, nodding.

"Well, that surprises me."

"It does, dear?"

"I always liked that clock."

Good Lord, would she want it back?

Louise sighed. "But on the other hand, I'm *not* surprised."

"You aren't, dear?"

"So *many* things have been disappearing around here lately."

"Like what?"

The woman made a lemon-sucking face. "*Money*, for one! And a gold necklace. That's why I hardly ever leave my apartment anymore. Why don't they have locks on these doors, anyway?"

I said, "I suppose it's because the staff needs to get in quickly, should one of us have an accident or medical emergency. Any idea who the bandit might be?"

Another sour face twisted her mouth. "I have a suspicion. That orderly . . . or is he a janitor? Anyway, that man who always comes in every morning, to empty the wastebasket."

"I believe his name is Blake Ferrell."

"I wouldn't know," she snapped. "He's someone whose acquaintance I'd rather not make. And he never knocks! And sometimes I'm napping in the bedroom! What if I were deshabille?"

What part of her failing memory had she pulled that one out of?

As if on cue, a knock came at the door and, without the knocker waiting for the knockee's permission, it opened, and the gentleman of whom we'd been speaking came tromping in. Perhaps in his midtwenties, Blake Ferrell had dark hair and needed a shave—fashion statement or slovenliness, who can say these days?—and his clothes consisted of a plaid shirt, blue jeans, and sneakers. He might have been good-looking, if it weren't for his sullen, scruffy countenance.

The janitor moved past us without even a glance. We might have been part of the furniture.

"See?" Louise huffed, loud enough for the young man to hear. "Doesn't even knock, just walks right in."

Well, he *had* knocked, but not loud enough for a senior citizen with fading aural powers to pick up.

I could hear him rustling around in the kitchen, then he reemerged hauling a black plastic garbage bag, and went out as quickly and wordlessly as he'd come in.

Louise picked up where she'd left off. "It's not *right* for a man to enter a woman's apartment when she's sleeping. I told Harriet and she promised to bring it up with Mr. Burnett . . . but then she got blown to smithereens, and I'm right back where I started."

The woman was getting more and more agitated, so I shifted subjects. "Dear, is it true that you got bedsores here so badly you nearly lost a leg?"

I'd barely got this out when I realized this might not be a calming query.

She shifted in her recliner and frowned. "Nonsense! Never happened."

Either Alice had been wrong, or Louise couldn't remember.

"But I did have shingles on my leg," she said, "that got so infected I might've lost it."

So Alice, like a clock without a minute hand, had been half right.

I said, "Surely the doctor here, making rounds, must have looked at it."

"Yes, and ordered up some ointment to put on it. But do you think I could get anyone to help me apply it? They were always too busy!"

"Did you happen to mention this to Harriet?"

Her laugh was a cackle. "Sure did! And I bet she cost this dump a fine over that, or at least some kind of reprimand."

Sensing I'd gotten about all the information I could from Louise, I took my leave.

My final stop of the morning was at the end of the corridor—the apartment of Arthur Fillmore, a retired insurance agent who also eschewed morning exercise, sing-songing, and artsy-crafting.

"Vivian, come in, come in!" Arthur greeted me.

Arthur reminded me of the old stage and screen actor Lionel Barrymore—not much to look at, perhaps, but charismatic and confident. His wife was a gentle, lovely lady among the angels now, although she must have already been one here on earth to put up with her hubby's dalliances. But time had slowed the randy old goat down somewhat . . . or so I thought. . . .

I wheeled into a sparse but messy front room, newspapers and magazines littering the floor, where also resided more than a few dirty plates that should have long since been carted off to the kitchen.

Arthur helped me position myself across from his recliner before he sat, though did not lean back.

A television was playing loudly nearby and—when my host made no move to turn it down (or preferably off)—I did what I always do in that situation: I began to speak very softly, which made him ask me to repeat myself, which

I did, but even softer (sometimes I just move my lips). Finally Arthur got up and turned off the intrusive boob tube, although it was actually a small flat-screen.

Returning to his recliner, he asked, "I suppose you've come about the title to the car?"

"No," I said in my normal, if stage-trained, voice. "But have you found it?"

"I have."

"Then I'll take it before I leave." I shifted in the hard wheelchair, wishing I'd sought a cushion to rest upon.

I opened with Cora Van Camp's tidbit. "Arthur, what do you know about any employees here at Sunny Meadow who have past criminal records?"

He shrugged. "I have no firsthand knowledge . . . only what Harriet shared with me."

"Which was?"

"That she had proof and was going to confront Mr. Burnett about it. You know, with a deputy sheriff as a nephew, she couldn't just be shrugged off."

"Did she say *what* proof she had?"

"Sorry, no."

"Or mention any names?"

He shook his head. "But I agreed with her that a nursing home would be easy pickings for someone with a criminal bent, and that person might make less than an ideal employee."

I then asked Arthur about Harriet smoking around her oxygen tank, but he said with his apartment being at the end of the hall, he was unaware of her habits.

He went on: "I did notice one thing . . . different . . . about the morning Harriet died. When I stepped out into the hall to retrieve my morning paper, I saw Joan—the head nurse?—going into Harriet's apartment about seven-thirty with a tank of oxygen."

"What was different about that?" I asked.

"Well, that was *Wanda's* job," Arthur said. "At least it always was in the past."

I nodded. "Because she brings around whatever is prescribed, which includes oxygen."

"Right."

Then out of nowhere, my host said, "You know, Vivian, if you don't mind my frankness, I've always thought you were just about the most attractive woman in town."

Not wanting to encourage him, I demurred, "Close only counts in horseshoes."

He crawled out of the recliner and stood before me. "Oh, no. Even now. Why, you haven't aged a day."

I could hardly say the same thing about him.

The old goat leaned down, and at first I thought he'd snapped his fingers, like Edd "Kookie" Byrnes, but it was only a backbone popping.

He said slyly, "Maybe you could come back later this evening and we could see about me turnin' over that car title to you . . . for your white elephant sale."

I didn't want to win *that* badly!

I said, "You *do* see these two casts on my feet."

He winked. "You know, there's always a work-around, little lady."

I smiled up at him, calling upon all my thespian skills. "I do so love a challenge. Shall we say . . . eight?"

He grinned, showing off dentures as white and gleaming as a freshly scrubbed toilet bowl. "Eight it is, dolly."

The man could wait till half past doomsday, and I still wouldn't show up.

I made my escape.

I'm going to do a little rant here, dear reader, and not about sexual contact among residents in nursing homes. For heaven's sake! We're all of age. Why not have a little thrill on the way to the great beyond? As long as it's consensual, that is. But Arthur Fillmore just didn't trip my trigger.

No, my beef is when people begin a sentence with, "You know . . ." Well, I *don't* know. Not until that person tells me what they're going to say, and then maybe I do know, or don't. This verbal idiosyncracy is spreading like a most unwelcome rash. You know?

Where was I?

I was wheeling toward the elevator when my cell phone rang. I usually power it off when I'm investigating, not wanting any interruption in my train of thought, but I must have gone off the track and forgotten to do so.

The caller was Brandy.

"Mother," she began. "How can I get in touch with Judd Pickett's daughter?"

This threw me. "*Della* Pickett? But why, dear?"

"Never mind. I'll fill you in later."

"Well, all right. I believe she still works at that artists' gallery on Fourth Street. Dear, can't you give me a reason?"

But she said, "In a hurry!" And ended the call.

Now my mind would be cluttered with worry and wondering for hours until the girl arrived. Some people can be so thoughtless! All one can do is set a good example and hope.

I took the elevator to the second floor, and when I rolled off, there down the hallway stood Deputy Dugan, poised at the door to my room. I watched him go inside, then immediately come out, perhaps expecting me to be within. But why didn't he knock?

Wheeling toward him, I called out, "Oh, yoohoo!"

He turned, frowned, smiled mildly, and approached me.

"Were you looking for me, Deputy Dugan?" I asked. "Or are you out here on some other mission?"

"Both, really. My aunt had some clothes down in the laundry room at the time of the accident, and I thought a few of the patients on welfare could use them. So I gave my permission."

"How nice."

He went on, "And while I was here, I wanted to see how you were getting on."

"Peachy keen," I said. "But I notice you entered my quarters without knocking—not that I expect you to be packing a warrant or anything!"

"I was afraid you might be sleeping. You know, I have to admit I was a little thrown by the timing of your surgery."

"Oh?"

"To be off the campaign trail for a week or more *could* cost you."

"Oh, I don't think so," I countered. "Most people don't pay attention to the election until about a month before the vote."

He gave me a polite smile and lifted a forefinger. "Don't forget, we have a forum in front of the city council at their next meeting."

It had slipped my mind; but that was a few weeks away.

"Of course, I remember! But it's nice of you to remind me, nonetheless. Honor among candidates and all."

"Well, I hope you'll be able to be there."

My grin may have been a trifle too wide. "With rings on my fingers and bells on my newly aligned toes, I will!"

He nodded, then frowned. "By the way, Mrs. Rockwell reported a clock missing. I know she's forgetful, so there's probably nothing to it."

"Sorry, dear, can't help you with that," I replied, and rolled on, calling jokily over my shoulder, "I'm not sheriff yet!"

In my room, I got out of the wheelchair and into the bed

myself, even though I was not supposed to. It took some wiggling, but that was better than waiting for Wanda to come and help.

Using my room phone, I called the cafeteria to have a late lunch brought to me, instead of making the trip there. The mixture of smells from all the food options was rather off-putting; besides, I thought I'd take a short snooze while waiting for the grub.

Sometime later, I awoke to find my tray had been delivered. Hungry, the chocolate babka having worn off, I was about to dig in when I noticed a folded piece of paper tucked beneath the plate.

The hand-lettered note read: *MEET ME IN THE GARDEN AT 3 PM IF YOU WANT TO KNOW WHAT'S GOING ON.*

Did I? I always want to know what's going on!

I looked at the clock next to Gabby Hayes. Good Lord—three p.m. was in just five minutes! I had really conked out. Demon babka!

Quickly I switched from the bed to the wheelchair, and rolled out of my room, heading for the elevator to go down, and then outside.

The garden was a secluded spot enclosed by tall evergreen bushes, with a variety of flowers, and cement benches, overseen by a life-size statue of an angel with wings, resembling faintly if coincidentally Arthur's late wife. This area was mostly used by visitors, a quiet place for them to escape the nursing home and come to grips with the reality of their loved ones' new lives.

Because stone steps led down to the garden, my only option to get there was via a path off the steep driveway. This might have intimidated some, but not me—should I get going too fast, I was no novice at using the brakes on a wheelchair. After all, I had played Sheridan Whiteside in my all-female version of *The Man Who Came to Dinner.*

(Though perhaps I should have retitled it *The Woman Who Came to Dinner*, and not worn the beard.)

Unfortunately, I had never had a need until now to test the brakes on my current ride, and very quickly found that they didn't work at all well. The bolts were too loose for the little metal plates to press properly against the wheels!

I flew past the garden path, staying on the driveway but not by choice, hit a speed-bump, and suddenly the left wheel shot off its axle. Then, tilting the chair to the right, balancing on a single wheel like a circus monkey on a unicycle, I was following the remaining wheel's mate down the drive, ever picking up speed, trying to stay balanced while Fourth of July sparks flew from the metal frame's contact with the cement. I said a little prayer as I headed onto the highway, and turned unwillingly into the path of an oncoming car.

Mother's Trash 'n' Treasures Tip

Sometimes white elephant attendees are sneaky and will hide an item they want in an area where it doesn't belong, either to come back for it later, or wait until the last hour when prices might drop. So check out all sections. I've had success burying women's jewelry among men's tools.

Chapter Six

Buffalo Bilious

With Mother tooling around Sunny Meadow Manor in her special wheelchair, "looking into things," I would likely be hearing soon from Mr. Burnett, complaining about her upsetting the natural state of affairs at the nursing home—as if there were anything *I* could do about it.

For Sushi and me, with our day quiet and a little boring without Mother around, our first responsibility was the shop, although I could tell about an hour after opening that business was going to be slow. The weather was just too perfect—sunny and midseventies—and people were more inclined to be outside doing something fun today than wandering inside an antique store looking at yesterdays.

I wondered for a moment if I should drag a table of merchandise into the front yard to catch the eye of the occasional pedestrians strolling or jogging by. But, like them, it passed.

Sushi liked to follow customers around and would stop when they paused in their shopping and stare up at them, possibly giving the impression she'd been trained to bark or growl at any sign of shoplifting. Actually, there were a handful of regulars who brought along treats for her and had unwittingly trained her to do this. I was convinced a real shoplifter could pocket a thousand-dollar necklace (if we had one) as long as he brought Sushi a doggie biscuit.

Today she was taking the lack of foot-traffic in stride, curled up in her leopard-print bed on the floor behind the counter. I was keeping busy at the computer, preparing a monthly sales report (down), from which Mother and I could see what was trending (miniature oil paintings, cast-iron doorstops, vinyl records), and what was not (fine china, figurines, Bakelite jewelry).

I was also noting merchandise we'd had for a long time that we should try harder to sell, or else be stuck with (yellow "smiley face" alarm clock, lacquered fruitcake wreath—my mistakes; glass insulators, old typewriter—Mother's miscalculations).

All of that done, I decided to clean out some files that were collecting dust in a box beneath the counter. One file contained old notices from the police department regarding stolen property, circulated to pawnshops and antiques dealers to be on the lookout for. These usually covered high-end items like diamonds and Rolex watches, well out of our buying price range, or modern electronics that we didn't deal in, so truthfully we never paid much attention to the notices. (Pawnshops and dealers now can consult several online databases if they suspect something is stolen.)

I leafed through the papers and was about to toss them in the wastebasket, when a name caught my eye—Judd Pickett. Listed as missing from his home after his death were two objects—first, a Bowie knife with unpolished blade, ten and one-half inches long and two inches wide, with a three-inch-long clip, iron guard, and a handle made of wood held together by brass rivets. Second, an Indian peace pipe with long spiral stem, carved raised rings decorated by brass tacks, and a catlinite bowl.

Checking the website of a local funeral home listing all area deaths going back years, I found the date of Mr. Pickett's demise, which coincided with the date on the police notice.

An online article by a *Serenity Sentinel* reporter didn't reveal much information about Pickett's murder, probably because the PD didn't want details released since the perp hadn't been apprehended.

But I knew where *I* might get those details. . . .

I reached for my cell and sent Tony a text: *How about lunch with a beautiful blonde?*

He got right back to me: *Can do, at 11.*

Me: *Have food here at the shop.*

Him: *OK.*

I hopped off my stool.

You remember me mentioning that we had a functioning kitchen at the shop? With vintage appliances, dishes, pots and pans, silverware, old cookbooks, even a red-topped Formica table with red vinyl chairs, all for sale. The only thing that wasn't old—or for sale—was the refrigerator where we kept our cookie dough and grub. We had made the mistake of having a cool 1950s white Philco fridge, and as soon as we'd stocked it with food for ourselves, someone came in and bought the darn thing!

I set about getting lunch ready.

Before her bunion operation, Mother had made several casseroles at home and frozen them there—not with my welfare in mind, but because she thought the food at Sunny Meadow might be not to her liking. Having thawed one and brought it along today, I popped it into the 1970s avocado-green oven (no buyer interest in that appliance—nostalgia hadn't caught up with it yet).

Mother's Easy Chicken Casserole

1 4-oz. package dried beef
4 chicken breasts, skin removed
4 slices uncooked bacon
2 cups uncooked instant rice
1 can undiluted mushroom soup
1 8-oz. carton sour cream

Spread rice in the bottom of a buttered 9-x-13-inch baking dish. Cover with layer of dried beef. Combine the soup and sour cream, then spread over dried beef. Wrap bacon around chicken breasts, and place on top. Cover and cook at 250 degrees for about two hours.

I would throw together a Bibb lettuce salad at the last minute, and serve yesterday's chocolate-chip cookies for dessert.

While the casserole was warming, I got the coffee going, then set the table for two with colorful Fiestaware dishes, and yellow Bakelite-handled silverware. Sushi, hearing the clattering, roused herself and trotted in, knowing that food was in her future. Not for a second had she thought a burglar had broken in requiring her watchdog powers.

Promptly at eleven, Tony arrived, and I went to greet him, putting a CLOSED sign on the door, so we wouldn't be disturbed. Without Mother around, who knew what might transpire?

"Something smells good," the chief said.

"Ever the detective," I said.

He was sans navy blazer for a change, the sleeves of his light blue shirt rolled, and wearing the usual tan slacks, with badge clipped to his belt, and brown Florsheim shoes. Summer was almost here and our chief of police looked recklessly casual.

Hearing her (and my) master's voice, Sushi left her vigilant guard duty over the casserole in the kitchen, came scampering, and practically leapt into Tony's arms. (The Borne girls are not known for their propriety where matters of the heart are concerned.)

While Soosh adored my guy, Rocky—the chief's mutt with a rakish black circle around one eye—was the real love of her life, and she could probably smell his scent on Tony's clothes.

He gave her some attention, then put her down.

I gave him a curled finger and he followed me into the kitchen, Sushi so close on his heels he might have been a police car.

Soon we were enjoying a crisp salad, a steaming casserole, and hot coffee. I'd opened a nearby window and a gentle breeze drifted in to ruffle the white cotton curtains.

"And how is your day?" I asked, like we were a long-married couple sitting down for lunch in our own little bungalow kitchen.

Tony swallowed a bite of casserole. "Hectic, so I can't stay long—say, this is delicious."

"Don't sound so surprised."

Usually, when I cooked for Anthony Cassato, I made Italian dishes, so I confessed the work was Mother's.

"How is she?" he asked. Whether that was concern or just politeness, it was nice of him to ask, considering that she was a bigger pain to him than her bunions had been to her.

I told him the casts would come off her feet in a few weeks, and then she'd be home from Sunny Meadow and back on the campaign trail.

He had a little smile going. "I still don't see why now of all times she finally got around to doing something about her legendary bunions. Was she planning on chasing perps on foot?"

I shrugged. "Rudder sometimes did." I didn't mention her ulterior motive of gaining access to possible murder witnesses and even suspects out at Sunny Meadow.

I studied Tony for a moment, picking up a worried vibe that I didn't think had a thing to do with her foot surgery. "Something wrong?"

"I mean . . . what if she wins?"

My casserole-loaded fork stopped in midair. "You can't be serious. You *know* that's impossible."

He smirked. "Impossible? If I've learned *anything* about Vivian Borne, it's not to underestimate her—with her, nothing is impossible."

"Look, Deputy Dugan is way ahead in the polls," I said, gesturing with the fork, my prospective bite flying onto the floor, where an ever-watchful Sushi gobbled it up.

"Those opinion phoners the *Serenity Journal* tallies up?" Tony said, with a mild smirk. "Not exactly the Gallup or Quinnipiac."

"Besides," I said, shrugging that off, "Dugan's way more qualified for the job."

His smirk remained. "Aren't you forgetting a certain presidential election?"

"Well, let's hope qualifications still matter on the local level." But now he had *me* worried. "I guess you'll miss having a colleague like Rudder to work with."

"Pete was—still *is*—a damn good sheriff."

"Will Dugan make a good sheriff, you think?"

". . . I'm sure he'll be fine."

That slight hesitation spoke volumes.

But I knew not to press; the chief was loyal to others in local law enforcement, and if he had qualms about Dugan, he'd keep them to himself. Trash talk was not his way—a continual frustration to Mother.

After the meal, and some small talk that's none of your business, I cleared the plates and served the cookies.

Nibbling on one (cookie, not plate), I asked him, ever so casually, to tell me about Judd Pickett.

He sat back and eyed me suspiciously. "Well, didn't *that* come out of nowhere."

"I ran across an old police 'Stolen Property' notice with his name, and since the murder happened before I moved back to Serenity, I thought maybe you could answer some questions."

"What sparks your interest in such an old case? Somebody try to sell you items from Pickett's collection?"

He *would* ask. "No. It's probably nothing. Mother has it in her head that Harriet Douglas was murdered. . . ."

"Oh please."

". . . and Harriet gave Mother a photograph of Gabby Hayes that—"

"You kind of lost me at Gabby Hayes."

"He was a sidekick of Roy Rogers and—"

"I *know* who he was." His eyes widened, then closed, then opened, tentatively. "So Harriet gave your mother a photo of Gabby Hayes. Go on."

"It was autographed, and it was from the Judd Pickett collection. So if she's right, and Harriet was murdered, here's another murder, unsolved, from years ago, with Pickett turning up again."

"I'm afraid your mother has been a bad influence on you, sweetheart. Pickett wasn't murdered, he was killed."

"There's a difference?"

"Well, of course he *was* murdered, but . . . Pickett was a casualty in a home invasion. It wasn't a premeditated Agatha Christie kind of thing."

I thought for a moment. "Was the knife or peace pipe mentioned in that circular ever found?"

"No. Nor was the killer ever caught—but why do I think you already know that?"

I decided not to answer—it sounded rhetorical. "What *did* happen? The newspaper didn't report much."

What Tony told me was this: widower Judd Pickett came home early one evening from a weekly bingo game, apparently surprised an intruder, who panicked and hit the old man with a fireplace poker, killing him instantly. A woman who happened to be driving by saw a ski-masked figure running from the house and called 911.

"Then you arrived?" I asked.

Tony shook his head. "The housing development where Pickett lived was in the sheriff's jurisdiction . . . although that area has since been incorporated into the city, which puts the cold case in *my* lap."

I could tell having an unsolved murder lingering out there bothered Tony. Murder was enough of a rarity in a small town that few went unresolved. Especially since Mother started getting involved.

I asked, "Was the witness able to give a description of the intruder?"

"Not really," Tony said with a sigh. "It was night, the perp wore black—of a size and frame slight enough to have been male or female."

"I bet it was a young man."

"Oh?"

"Mr. Pickett had all kinds of valuables, and what did the killer take? A knife and a pipe—what, a knife as a weapon, a pipe to smoke dope?"

Tony nodded. "Could be."

"You know . . ." (Sorry, Mother.) ". . . enough time has gone by that those items just might surface."

"Been known to happen," Tony said with another nod. "Perp might think it's safe now, and be stupid enough to want a few bucks for 'em. Not that items like that would get him or her anything but pocket money."

"Who reported the knife and pipe missing?"

"Pickett's daughter." Tony checked his watch. "Sorry, honey, but I've got to go. If you want to know more, you might try asking Rudder." He chuckled. "But I doubt, with his history with you and your mother, that he'll be forthcoming. After all, you won't be bribing *him* with chicken casserole and chocolate-chip cookies."

"I've had nicer thank-yous for lunch."

He got up, leaned over, and gave me a slightly chocolately kiss. "Are you sure?"

I accompanied Tony to the door, where he slipped his arms around my waist.

"So," he said lightly. "When exactly are we going to get married, anyway? Haven't changed your mind, have you?"

"Of course not! Only . . . I'd like to wait till after the election. Mother's pretty much certain to lose, and she *could* take it hard."

"She might go reeling at that," he admitted.

"When her life calms down, we can get serious about tying the knot."

His smile was sad. "Brandy, Vivian Borne's life *never* calms down. You know that."

He chuckled to himself, kissed me on the forehead, and left.

I relocked the door, then returned to the counter where I reached Mother on her cell.

"Mother," I asked, "how can I get in touch with Judd Pickett's daughter?"

"*Della* Pickett? But why, dear?"

"Never mind. I'll fill you in later."

"Well, all right. I believe she still works at that artists' gallery on Fourth Street. Dear, can't you give me a reason?"

"In a hurry!" I said, and ended the call.

I got my purse, picked up Sushi, locked up, and headed out.

The gallery—a retail shop where local artisans consigned everything from jewelry to pottery to photography and more—was one of several businesses in a former funeral home, an old, white, stucco, two-story structure with phony facades and fake balconies lending it an eerie aura of unreality.

I'd only been inside the building once, to visit the clock repair shop run by the owner of the building, Mr. Timmons, who rented out the four visitation rooms. His shop was in back, housed in the one-time "preparation room" (feel free to shudder) where the man blithely used the ancient embalming tables as workbenches (and shiver).

I had avoided the art gallery till now, not so much due to the structure's creepy atmosphere, but because I felt that when I stopped by a shop like this, I should really purchase something. I mean, I knew what it was like to run a shop, and have a potential customer come in and get your hopes up, before dashing them.

And between Mother and me, we already had enough stuff in our house (and our garage, which hadn't had room for a vehicle in recent memory) that buying anything that wasn't an antique earmarked for Trash 'n' Treasures resale just didn't make sense.

The gallery was in the first grieving parlor to the left, and I entered the spacious room with Sushi in my arms. She was sniffing some ghost of terrible fluids that still faintly floated through the rooms.

Glass display counters, curios, and Grecian exhibit columns helped disguise the origin of the space, but a few telltale signs remained, such as the small alcoves for urns and church-like stained-glass windows.

A middle-aged woman appeared from behind a heavy velvet curtain in a back corner, approached, then asked pleasantly, "May I help you?"

Fashionably dressed in a pale pink suit with gold buttons and beige patent leather pumps, she had a nice figure and sleek shoulder-length brown hair, making the most of her attributes because, unfortunately, she had inherited the angular face of her father, as seen in the obit.

I introduced myself.

"I know who you are," Della said with a smile. "Your mother and my father were old friends."

How old and how friendly? I had long since learned not to inquire about such things.

She asked, "Is there a particular artist or item you're interested in?"

"There are a lot of lovely things here," I said, not lying (entirely), "but I'm hoping you might be willing to let me ask you a few questions about what happened to your father."

Her expression registered surprise, then clouded. "Well, what happened to my father was that he was murdered."

I nodded awkwardly.

She said, "I suppose everyone in town knows that you and your mother have a . . . an unusual *hobby*, looking into this sort of thing. But I guess I don't mind talking to you. Why don't you give me a call—I'll give you my cell number."

"I thought maybe . . ."

"You mean here? *Now?*"

I glanced uncomfortably around—tumbleweed.

"Well . . ." I said.

Della gestured with a flip of a hand. "Never mind. Now

is fine. You and your cute little dog are the first customers I've had today, and talking to anybody, even about *that*, will break things up a little. But let's sit."

She led me to a pair of chairs that had been splashed with glistening, colorful paint. "I use these for the husbands of wives that're looking," she said. "Not a lot of guys are into local arts and crafts, unless they make them themselves."

"I can imagine," I said, as we sat.

I settled Sushi on my lap, fully expecting to rise with a rainbow of paint smears and a sprinkling of sparkles on my behind.

"Now," Della said, as pleasantly businesslike as if I really were a customer, "why do you want to know about Dad? The police seemed to abandon the case ages ago. Has something new come to light?"

"Not that I know of," I admitted.

"Oh," she replied disappointedly.

I went on, "But I am curious about a few things, if you don't mind."

"Not at all," she said. "Especially if you and Vivian get involved. With the police off the case, you'd be . . ." I think she was about to say "better than nothing," but instead she added: ". . . welcome."

"I can't promise anything. It's just an unsolved killing with a vague connection or two to the recent death of Harriet Douglas."

"That was accidental, wasn't it?"

"Well, Mother has her doubts. But again, I don't want to get your hopes up."

Della nodded. "I understand. You're both busy with the upcoming election—she has my vote, by the way."

"Mother will appreciate that," I replied. People were continually saying that to me, and I was always surprised. I wasn't even sure *I'd* vote for her, and I was her campaign manager.

Della settled back in the chair. "So. What do you want to know?"

"I understand your dad had a big collection of western memorabilia. Was there an inventory that told you only a knife and pipe were taken?"

"No. I wish there had been, but Dad was such an inveterate collector, his personal museum was always on the grow."

"Yet you felt it was only those two items."

"I suppose there could have been other things. But I saw Dad that morning and he had those two pieces set out on the table. He'd mentioned he was going to contact the Buffalo Bill Museum in Wyoming about donating them. Well, Dad wouldn't have had time to make the arrangements, let alone send them off."

I frowned. "If they were museum quality, they must have been worth something . . . but the police circular didn't mention values."

Pickett's daughter shifted in her chair. "No. I didn't let out what they were worth for fear of never getting them back." She paused, obviously weighing whether or not to share more with me, and then did: "The knife, in fact, had belonged to James Bowie himself—one of the few known. And the peace pipe was similarly significant, having been given to Buffalo Bill by Chief Sitting Bull."

"Good heavens," I gasped. "*Insured*, I hope."

"Afraid not. Dad had a funny attitude about insurance. Nearly everything in his collection was irreplaceable—one of a kind—and he felt that if something was lost or stolen, what good would the insurance money do? He couldn't buy the exact same thing again. Besides, the premiums would have been sky high."

Mother harbored the same attitude about insurance—maybe it was a generational thing. I had to make sure the car, house, and shop always had coverage.

I asked, "If your father didn't keep an inventory of his collectibles, how about a record of what he bought and sold?"

Della shook her head. "Any time Dad would sell something, it would be for cash. He *never* wrote out a receipt. What the buyer got with the item was a letter of provenance written by Dad giving a description of that item, where it came from, and his signature. Then when he sold or traded it, he would add a sentence that its ownership was being transferred to so-and-so, and sign that."

"No mention of what money exchanged hands?"

Della shook her head. "And, remember, sometimes he was trading for another rare item, not buying. A collector might have to give something more precious than what he or she is after, to shake an item loose from another hardcore collector."

I knew all about that kind of thing. I said, "I understand your father sold Daryl Dugan a particularly rare Wyatt Earp poster."

"Yes. I didn't know about that. In fact, Dad parting with the poster surprised me, because he only got it a year before he died. On the other hand, he and Daryl were close, what with their mutual interest. But shortly after Dad's death, Daryl dropped by my house, concerned—we both live in Stoneybrook—to make sure I knew the transaction was legitimate."

"He showed you the letter of provenance?"

She nodded. "It was in Dad's handwriting, I'm sure of that, saying Daryl was now the owner." She paused, then added, "Even though Dad's writing had gotten a little shakier with age, it was definitely his."

"Would your father have deposited a large sum of cash into a bank account around that time?"

She laughed. "I told you how Dad felt about insurance—take a wild guess how he felt about paying income tax on collectibles he'd sold."

"What did he do with the cash?"

"Wall safe."

Most likely what the intruder was after.

Della was saying, "And yes, it was still loaded with money—the thief must have been interrupted, or lacked safe-cracking skills. But I couldn't tell you where any of it came from."

We fell into silence.

Then I said, "I don't think I have anything else. I hope I haven't caused you too much pain."

"It still hurts," she admitted. "Losing a loved one is never easy, and Dad was no spring chicken, as he'd have put it. But dying like that?" She shook her head. "And I miss Dad every day."

I thanked the woman for her time, and left.

The afternoon was still young, so I decided to pay a visit to Serenity's oldest established hock shop, From Pawn to King, which occupied the first floor of a restored redbrick Victorian building on Main Street.

Every so often, Mother and I could snag an undervalued antique there, put out on the floor after nonpayment of a loan. But such bargains were becoming increasingly rare— over 80 percent of people pay back their loans and reclaim their property, plus the shop's owner, Mr. McElroy, had begun concentrating his trade mostly on electronics, sports gear, guitars, tools, and jewelry (he didn't deal in guns).

I left an unhappy Sushi in the car, windows cracked, and entered the barred-windowed pawnshop, an electronic buzzer announcing my arrival. Mr. McElroy—who used to run a junk shop back when junk was just that—was busy sorting a stack of DVDs behind a glass counter, and looked up.

He was an ex-Marine, having served in the Korean War, and still looked formidable with his white crew cut, thick neck, and stocky but still muscular trunk stretching the fabric of a black T-shirt with store logo. Anyone would think twice before tangling with him.

"Well, Brandy," he said. "I'd been meaning to call you and Vivian. I'm stuck with an old milkshake mixer that I know won't sell with my crowd."

"Hamilton Beach?" I asked.

He nodded. "Green. One spindle. Interested?"

I was very interested. The vintage mixer would go great in our shop's kitchen, and if we couldn't unload it, I could always make myself a malt on the coming hot summer days!

But I knew not to look too excited.

I shrugged, then fibbed, "Vintage kitchen electronics haven't been selling for us, either." Big sigh. "But go ahead and send us a photo, and I'll have Mother take a look at it." She was the horse trader. "You have our shop's e-mail?"

He did.

"Mr. McElroy . . ." I began.

"Brandy, I think we've known each other long enough for you to call me Tom."

"Tom."

"What's on your mind, girl, besides gyping me out of that mixer?"

"You knew Judd Pickett?"

"Sure did. Nice fellow. Terrible what happened."

I'd brought along the police notice of the missing knife and peace pipe, and slid the paper on the counter toward him. "Do you remember seeing this?"

Tom picked the notice up, ran his eyes over it.

"Vaguely," he said, frowning. "Mostly I recall thinking these items were nothing I'd be interested in either loaning money on or buying."

"You might have thought different if you'd known what they really were."

"Huh?"

I told him.

Tom emitted a long, low whistle. "I knew Judd had some valuable western stuff . . . but, good Lord! Why was *this* kept a secret?"

I gave him Della's reasoning that the knife and pipe might surface if no one—including the killer—knew their worth.

I asked, "Wasn't there another pawnshop in town for a while?"

"Out of business," he said. "The pawn trade is tough, what with all the regulations—federal, state, *and* local."

"What happened to their stock?" I asked.

"I bought it for peanuts. Mostly crap, which tells me why they went out of business." He gestured with his head toward the back of the store. "It's still in boxes I haven't had time to go through."

"How soon might you get around to that?"

"With valuable western antiques like that maybe back there? Pretty darn quick. Don't worry, I won't pull anything. I didn't stay in business this long dealing in stolen property."

"You don't have to convince me."

"But, Brandy, less than one tenth of one percent of stolen items ever turn up in pawnshops."

"I know. Because of the photo ID that's required, and the databases that can be checked."

Tom gestured to the police notice. "I'll take a picture of this, just in case." Which he did with his cell phone, then handed me back the paper.

I thanked him and left.

When I got into the car, Sushi, in the passenger seat,

wouldn't look at me. She hated to be left behind, even for a short time.

So I said, "Let's go out to Sunny Meadow and see Mother," a sentence that had two words she loved to hear—*go*, and *Mother*.

Soon we were tooling south along scenic Mississippi Drive, the river to our left sparkling in the afternoon sun, a strong breeze making little whitecaps. A big barge loaded with cargo—probably grain—was making its way slowly downstream, headed to destinations like Natchez and New Orleans. For some reason, I started whistling the theme to the old *Maverick* TV show.

Sushi crawled over and stuck her head out my powered-down window (I had a good grip on her) and the fur on her face flattened in the wind, pink tongue flapping to one side of her mouth.

Soon we were on the bypass, then making an exit into the majestic rolling hills. In a few minutes, Sunny Meadow came into view, perched high on one of those hills.

As I approached the entrance leading up the steep drive to the facility, a bicycle tire suddenly bounced across the road in front of the car, and I slammed on the brakes, thankful I had a good hold on Sushi.

At least, I had *thought* it was a bicycle tire until I saw what came next: a careening one-wheeled wheelchair carrying Mother, doing a balancing act that once upon a time could have gotten her on *The Ed Sullivan Show*.

Which back in the day was on opposite *Maverick*, which hardly seemed the point at the moment.

A Trash 'n' Treasures Tip

Check out all areas of a white elephant sale. Sometimes people carry around an item for a while, then decide against the purchase (or see something they like better) and abandon it where they happen to be. If someone has something in hand that Mother really wants, she will follow the person around in case that might happen. In that case, I find myself trailing her, humming the *Jaws* theme to myself. Softly.

Chapter Seven

Rollin', Rollin', Rollin'

With my windshield like a personal movie screen, I watched helplessly as the runaway wheelchair carrying Mother on a single wheel raced across the road, the single free-range tire bouncing down into the ditch.

Quickly, I pulled the C-Max off the highway, gave Sushi a command to stay inside, got a "who do you think you're talking to" look (but she obeyed), jumped out, and ran to the top of the ravine.

Mother was sitting at the bottom, in the tall grass, legs extended. To her left lay the single tire; to her right, the tipped-over wheelchair, attached wheel still spinning like a roulette wheel on the *Lady Luck* riverboat.

"*Mother!*" I cried, quickly descending. "Are you *all right*?"

She looked up. "Quite so, dear—thanks to a soft landing. Those Danish curves do come in handy, from time to time!"

I crouched next to her. She somehow looked both dazed and alert.

I said, "You shouldn't move until the ambulance comes."

She frowned. "You haven't *called* one, have you?"

My cell phone was poised in my hand. "Not yet."

"*Don't,*" she said firmly. "I'm fine. Let's not waste Medicare's money—they say it's going to run out in twenty years unless we're more frugal, and I plan on still being around."

Only Mother could worry about such things at a time like this.

Mr. Burnett appeared at the top of the embankment, as white as a ghost and as startled as if he'd just seen one. He came scurrying down toward us.

"My goodness," the overweight manager exclaimed, out of breath. "I saw the accident from my office window. Mercy sake! Has an ambulance been summoned?"

I rose from my crouch. "She doesn't want one."

Hands on hips, like a plump, capeless Superman, Burnett looked down at Mother. "Now, Mrs. Borne, you need to get checked out at the hospital. . . . We must make sure your feet weren't injured."

"My feet were well-protected in their casings," she retorted. "Furthermore, I feel fine—except for my posterior. There should have been more padding in the seat. Fortunately there was sufficient in mine."

To break the stalemate, I asked Burnett, "What if your head nurse examined her? And if she sees anything troubling, I'm sure Mother would agree to go to the hospital."

The man touched his chin. "Well . . . Joan is quite competent, so, yes—I would accept her evaluation."

"Mother?" I asked the still seated traveler. "Will you?"

She nodded.

This was Mother at her most devious. If the evaluation meant a trip to the ER, she would surely claim she'd never verbally agreed, and that her nod had been misinterpreted.

Burnett was saying, "I'll go make arrangements with the transport van."

As he huffed and puffed up the incline, possibly more in need of transport than Vivian Borne, I sat down in the grass with Mother.

Sushi had joined us, having heard the fuss (including Mother's voice), obviously disobeying my order by jumping out the car's open window. I pulled the little scoundrel onto my lap.

"Mother?"

"Yes, dear?"

"Can I ask you something?"

"But, of course." She stretched a hand out to pet Sushi, who made a sound as close to a purr as a canine can manage.

I squinted at her, as if that would help bring Vivian Borne into focus. "What were you thinking when you came sailing down the driveway and rolled across the road?"

"Well, I didn't do it on purpose, dear."

"No, I mean—what was going through your *mind*? I would have been screaming hysterically and my brain would have been filled with *oh-my-God, oh-my-God*."

"That does sound like you. Why do you ask?"

"Because you were *smiling*."

She beamed at the sky. "I believe you're right. I was thinking, if these are to be my last few minutes on earth, I may as well enjoy the ride. Just like the first time I jumped from an airplane and my parachute failed to open. Was I going to spend those final moments screaming in terror? *I should say not!* Why not know what it's like to skydive? Of course, then I remembered the emergency chute."

I had never heard this story, and had no idea she'd ever jumped from a plane, whether for fun or her life. But that didn't mean it didn't happen. I just wasn't going to go into it with her right now.

The transport van arrived and the two Manor men whose job was to take patients to medical appointments placed

Mother on a stretcher, then hauled her up the embankment. Yes, she was smiling again. Another new experience!

Sighing (I do that a lot around Mother), I returned to my car with Sushi and followed the van back up the driveway to Sunny Meadow.

This time, when I parked, I made sure the car's windows were only cracked open as I locked Sushi in.

I found Mother in her room, in bed, being examined by Nurse Joan Lindle, who took Mother's blood pressure, listened to her heart and lungs, checked eye movement and reflexes, and looked for broken bones and bruises.

The nurse's conclusion was that Mother appeared to be okay, but she recommended she go to the ER just to be on the safe side.

Naturally, the patient declined.

"Very well, I can't make you go," the nurse sighed. A lot of people sighed around Mother. "But I'm going to report my assessment to Mr. Burnett."

"Well, when that local doctor who makes afternoon rounds stops by, I'll fill him in. And tell Mr. Burnett I would sign off on anything he might require, to satisfy any fear of reprisal."

Mother knew her rights as a patient to refuse medical attention, even in a facility like this.

The nurse nodded in defeat and left.

I dragged the recliner up to the bed, and sat. "Well?"

"Well, what, dear?"

"What *happened*?" I asked, exasperated. "What were you *doing*?"

Mother told me about the anonymous note someone had given her, wanting to meet her in the garden, and said blithely that the only way she could get there in the wheelchair was by way of the steep drive.

I shook my head, rolled my eyes (I do a lot of both of

those around her, too). "And you didn't think to test the brakes beforehand?"

"Dear, I assumed the chair had been inspected before it was assigned to me. And, until then, I'd had no need to use the brakes in any meaningful fashion. Not a lot of steep slopes in a nursing home hallway!"

An unhappy-looking Mr. Burnett entered the room. "Mrs. Borne, I understand you're ignoring Joan's recommendation to go to the hospital."

"It was a suggestion," she said, "not a recommendation. And I said I'd sign off on whatever you deemed necessary."

"That's splitting hairs, Mrs. Borne," he said. "You're breaking your promise not to go gallivanting around, bothering the other patients."

Mother shrugged. "Why, did I nearly run one down?"

"Never mind that," I said to Burnett. "I want to know how my mother came to be given a wheelchair with defective brakes. And *nobody's* signing off on *that*."

Burnett put hands on hips again. "Miss Borne, your mother insisted on using that lightweight, extra-mobile chair, instead of one of our regular ones, even after I advised against it."

Extra-mobile was right. "You think that lets you off the hook?"

"Dear, stop badgering the man," Mother said. "I already *did* sign off—Mr. Burnett generously provided a paper absolving Sunny Meadow of any legal ramifications in order that I might use that wheelchair." She went on. "Besides, I'm tickety-boo. What occurred was merely happenstance."

"Well, you're not using that wheelchair again," I told her firmly. "Even if it gets fixed."

"No chance of that," Mr. Burnett told me. "It's been set

out for the trash." And to Mother, "You'll be given a standard one that will require someone to push you."

No more gallivanting.

"What about crutches?" Mother asked. "My doctor told me I could use them if I wanted."

The latter sounded credible, but it was untrue. Mother had a "tell," before uttering a lie: her eyes looked briefly to the right. (Left-handed fibbers look to the left.)

Burnett crossed to the window, looked out, paused, then turned, slightly distracted. "Very well, Joan can get you some crutches."

"That aren't defective," I said.

Burnett's smile oozed sarcasm. "I'll try to find a pair with limited moving parts."

When he'd gone, I asked Mother, "*Was* it an accident? Or did your snooping make someone so nervous they gave you that note, and tampered with the chair, knowing you'd likely get hurt—or worse?"

"Dear, you're letting your imagination get the best of you. I've learned very little on my unofficial rounds, certainly nothing that might make anyone nervous, let alone encourage a saboteur."

Another "tell," this one before being evasive: an ever-so-slight pursing of her lips.

I said, "Your very presence here is enough to cause concern for anyone who's got something to hide."

"Balderdash."

"Such language. But if what you say is right, you shouldn't mind telling me what you've been up to."

Mother sighed. "Very well, dear. This morning I went to see Mrs. Goldstein—she gave us the Vuitton suitcase, you'll recall."

"Yes, I recall. Go on."

"Well, she served up the most delicious chocolate babka I've ever had in my entire life. Not too sweet, with just the

right amount of lemon zest in the cake. And the fudge filling contained bittersweet chocolate, milk chocolate, *and*
cocoa—imagine that. Perfection! Although, personally, I
would have cut down a little on the kosher salt."

"All right. So you threw your diabetes paranoia to the
wind. But what did you *talk* about?"

Her eyes darted to the right. "Oh, not much . . . this and
that.

"Where did you go after that?"

"I paid Louise Rockwell a visit. She's the one who
gave us—"

"The clock, yes . . . stop stalling."

"Well, she was wearing the loveliest frock—red-and-
white checked material with white zigzag trim."

"Fascinating. What else?"

"Was she wearing?"

"Did you talk about!"

Mother's shrug would have seemed overstated in the
farthest back-row reaches of the Playhouse. "We discussed
the weather, and while we were doing so, young Blake Ferrell—he's the janitor—came in and emptied the kitchen
garbage can. A rather taciturn bloke."

She wasn't going to give me squat, and *bloke* meant her
faux Brit accent was threatening to break through—another facade for her to hide behind.

"Where did you go after that?" I asked.

"To see Arthur Fillmore, who—"

"Don't say it."

Mother huffed, "I wasn't going to say 'who offered us
that car.' I was going to say 'who told me something important that I didn't know.' "

I sat forward. Finally. "Really? What?"

She smiled girlishly. "Apparently Art has had a wild
crush on me for years. In fact, this morning he tried to make
a date with me for this evening, if you get my meaning."

I stood and, yes, sighed. "All right, Mother, keep your secrets. But I want you to come home. I can take care of you there, perfectly well. And Joe Lange can run the shop for a few weeks."

Joe was a friend I'd made during my one-year stint at Serenity Community College, an ex-marine who still lived with his widowed mother. Although suffering stress disorder from combat in the Middle East, he was competent enough to help us out from time to time.

"Speaking of the shop," Mother said, gesturing for me to sit back down, "how was your day?"

I just stood there. "Changing the subject won't help."

"Tell you what, dear. To ease your mind, why don't you leave Sushi with me for protection tonight? She's better than a can of mace and a rape whistle rolled into one. That Arthur, he was pretty darn frisky, earlier."

I tried to visualize what a mace-rape-whistle would look like. Better make sure to blow on the right end.

Actually, leaving Sushi with Mother wasn't a terrible idea. The little darling had come to our rescue more than once— Lassie in a smaller, cuter package. And I had trained her how to elude hotel staff when staying in "no pets" rooms, including scurrying under the bed. The circumstances here weren't much different.

Plus, if Mother got caught with a dog, Burnett would kick her out, and she'd be home where I could watch her.

"All right," I said. "I'll leave Sushi, and pick her up in the morning about eight."

Mother seemed pleased with herself. "Now, dear, I really am interested in your day at the shop."

I wasn't about to tell her anything, either, not when all I had was suspicions. Getting her thinking about the possibility of the Judd Pickett murder having some connection to Harriet's death would be like giving Sushi a single dog biscuit and thinking that would cover it.

"It was uneventful," I said, sitting back down, scratching my chin casually.

So I spoke of the lack of customers, plus the report I compiled showing we should buy more miniature oil paintings, cast-iron doorstops, and vinyl records; and shun fine china, figurines, and Bakelite jewelry.

Then, as we were running out of conversation, Mother seemed to be getting drowsy, and I thought it best to go. I went out to the car, got Sushi, made sure she piddled, got a blanket from the trunk, covered her with it, and returned to smuggle her in.

Sushi was ecstatic to be with her second mistress, who sleepily tucked Soosh away beneath the covers.

I kissed Mother on the cheek, told her I'd call later, and left a little before five.

But instead of heading straight for home, I drove around to the back of the building where a large dumpster sat. Piled next to it were the remains of the busted-up wheelchair.

I exited the car.

I could only examine the one brake on the tire that was still attached to the frame. And the bolts were indeed loose—not drastically so, but enough to make the contact of the metal tab against the tire ineffective.

On closer inspection, the bolts were also rusted, and some of the teeth on the screws looked stripped; so the mechanism could have come loose simply by Mother using the chair.

So it was maybe an accident, maybe not.

Cloaked in a feeling of unease, I got back into the car and drove away.

My darlings! Vivian is back. Yes, with another (half) chapter—what a lovely surprise, don't you think? Where shall I start . . . ?

First of all, I have to say how *very* excited I am about driverless cars, such as the Chevrolet Bolt—*buy American!*—which General Motors has been testing in Detroit, aka Motor City.

The autonomous vehicle will be especially helpful to those who have lost their driver's license (mostly through no fault of her own), and who will no longer have to resort to begging rides from friends, strong-arming lifts from relatives, or having to stoop to using unreliable forms of public transportation.

But I do have a few questions about the car.

1) Let's say, I'm in the self-driving car and it makes a violation all by itself. Will I be held responsible if I was busy putting on lipstick and not paying attention?
2) What if I give the car directions, and then, as we sail past Ingram's Department Store, I should happen to see a HALF-OFF SALE sign in the window. Just how quickly can the car make a U-turn?
3) Again, suppose I'm in the car and I mistakenly give it wrong directions, and we end up in a farmer's pasture, hitting a cow. Who pays for the cow? General Motors or an innocent driver who should have been protected by some technological fail-safe device? And if I do have to pay for the cow, can I have it transported to a meat locker facility?

(**Note to Vivian from Editor:** *Perhaps your queries would be better directed to a General Motors customer service representative.*)

(**Note to Editor from Vivian:** *You could be right! But someone out there reading this might already have the answers, and you know how difficult . . . nay, impossible . . . it is to get a real, live customer service representative from*

*any firm on the phone. And should it be a rep working out
of India, my question about the cow could prove upsetting.*)

(**Note to Vivian from Editor:** *Back on point, please.*)

I hated to keep pertinent details of my investigation
from Brandy, but I didn't see how the young woman could
be of any use to me at this early investigative juncture.
And, if I leveled with her about suspecting the wheelchair
had been tampered with, no telling *what* rash if well-
meaning action she might take.

Besides, I knew Brandy was keeping something from
me, when I asked about her day at the shop. She has a certain "tell" when she's not being truthful: she scratches her
chin.

Thankfully I have no such telltale mannerisms.

Anyhoo, after Brandy brought me Sushi, and I'd tucked
the fluffy darling away beneath the covers, I continued the
pretense of sleepiness, encouraging the girl to go home.

I had my dinner in my room, which came about five-
thirty—Sushi undetected now, beneath the bed—and I
shared the meat loaf dinner with her. Or, to be more pre-
cise, she shared it with me.

Afterward, a knock came to my door—Sushi jumping
from the bed to her hiding place beneath it—and Nurse
Wanda entered, pushing the pill cart, making her evening
rounds; she looked a little down in the dumps.

"Pain medication tonight, Mrs. Borne?" she asked rather
numbly, as if she were the one medicated.

"No need, dear," I said.

I really was aching from the "mishap," but didn't want
anyone to know, for fear I'd be shipped off to the ER.

"I heard about your accident," she said with all the enthusiasm of a waitress working the graveyard shift. "Glad
you're all right. How about something to help you sleep?"

"I am a bit keyed up, at that," I admitted. "But leave it with me—I'm not ready to retire so early. There's a mystery movie marathon on the Hallmark Channel."

With a flinch of a smile, Wanda placed a little white paper cup with two blue pills on the nightstand, then departed.

A little before seven, Nurse Joan came in—Sushi again scurrying beneath the bed, and just in time—bringing a pair of crutches, which she adjusted for my height, then set them against the wall right next to the bed.

"I'm off-duty now," she told me. "Wanda will be here during the night should you need anything."

I frowned. "Does that mean the poor girl will be doing a double shift?" Which would explain her less than cheerful demeanor.

Joan shrugged. "Yes. Can't be helped. Mr. Burnett is having trouble finding qualified nurses willing to work here at the rock-bottom pay he's offering." She sighed, then went on, "And when he *does* hire someone, they usually won't stay long—just until a better opportunity comes along. . . . Now, Vivian, you didn't hear that from me."

"Locked away in the vault, dear!" I cocked my head. "You and Wanda have been here quite a few years. I would imagine you both could have found a better opportunity."

"I'm used to it here," she replied. "Happy in my rut."

"And Wanda?"

"I can't speak for her. Well, good night, Mrs. Borne."

"*Au revoir.*"

I watched a little TV—why don't those Hallmark people make one of our books into a movie (probably they don't because we're writing true crime)—with Sushi snuggled by my side. Then I read a few chapters of *Death of a Dude* so that I'd be more informed for the next two or three Red Hatted League meetings.

Brandy called to check on me, and I told her everything was a-okay, and that I was about to get ready for bed.

After the call, I reached over and got the crutches, then made my way on the casts to the bathroom to brush my teeth (all mine, and I don't mean I paid for 'em). Sushi had come along to pee in the drain in the shower, which Brandy had taught her to do (not by example!), and it was as cute as it was unsanitary. Afterward I ran hot water with some soap, even though someone daily disinfected the bathroom.

(**Note to Vivian from Editor:** *Perhaps the reader doesn't need to know that Sushi relieved herself in the shower, which is a little off-putting.*)

(**Note to Editor from Vivian:** *Any dog owner is going to wonder why Sushi doesn't have to piddle for sixteen hours— from four in the afternoon, when Brandy brought her, until eight the next morning, when Brandy picks her up. Besides, those owners might appreciate the tip should they smuggle a dog into a no-pet room sometime. Hello? Are you still there?*)

After returning from the bathroom, I replaced the crutches and settled into bed with Sushi tucked beneath the covers by my side. I had decided not to take the sleeping pills because, why bother? I was already bone-tired—hurtling down a slope in an out-of-control wheelchair and crash-landing in a ravine takes it out of a gal—so I turned off the lamp and promptly fell asleep.

Sushi stirring woke me. The digital clock on the nightstand read a few minutes before the witching hour.

I had left a light on in the bathroom, the one above the sink, which allowed me to see across to where the horizontal silver handle of the room's door began to move slowly downward.

Since Wanda had no reason to be checking on me—this wasn't a hospital with vitals getting monitored ad infinitum—I sat up straight, like a horror show monster who turned out not to be dead. Sushi came out from beneath the covers, and sensing my trepidation, stood on the edge of the bed, eyes fixed on the door, a low growl rumbling in her throat.

The door eased open just enough for a figure to slip in.

As the person came toward me, Sushi sprang off the bed, hurtling herself through the air, landing at the intruder's feet, where she sank her sharp little teeth into a vulnerable ankle.

As the intruder howled, I turned on the lamp.

"Arthur!" I said, shocked. He was wearing a robe over striped pajamas.

"Get that filthy little beast off me," he cried.

"Sushi, come here," I commanded. "Now! And she's not filthy, and I think we both know who the *beast* here is."

Sushi trotted back to the bed and jumped up.

"Well?" I asked my uninvited guest. "Explain yourself."

"When you didn't show up," he said pitifully, rubbing the sore ankle, "I thought I'd better check on you."

"I had no intention of dropping by your quarters," I snapped. "And you had no right to come here unbidden. I am not playing Lucretia to your Tarquin!"

"I only wanted to give you the title to the car." He pitifully produced the paper from a pocket of the robe and wiggled the little title slip.

"That could have waited until morning," I said. "But, very well. Hand it over."

He did so, then—regaining some backbone—said indignantly, "You shouldn't have a dog in here. I could tell Burnett."

"I trust you won't. You'd have to explain to him exactly how it was that you found out. Good *night*, Arthur."

The man hesitated, then slipped back out.

"Good girl," I told Sushi, petting her head.

We settled again in bed, and I quenched the lamp.

I must admit I was the tiniest bit flattered by my midnight caller. A girl likes to be reminded at any age that she's still desirable (even if the one desiring her turns her stomach a bit).

Sushi and I went back to sleep.

I awoke again, acutely aware of a presence very near me.

"*Mr. Fillmore!*" I said reflexively. "I thought I made myself perfectly clear about your unwanted advances!"

But the figure was not Arthur, rather someone else— someone dressed in dark clothing and wearing a ski mask.

My outburst startled him—or her—and then came the sound of broken glass as something was knocked to the floor.

The intruder bolted.

Sushi was slow on the draw this time, burrowed at the bottom of the bed as she was, and before she could get to the person, he/she had fled, closing the door, preventing the dog from giving chase.

I switched on the lamp, which had not crashed to the floor. Nor had the clock, reading a quarter to three, lost its face. The casualty was the framed photo of Gabby Hayes, glass shards fanning out on the tile, Roy Rogers's sidekick grinning up at me, good as ever. Also just as toothless.

I pressed the call button to summon Wanda.

And waited.

And waited.

Finally, I eased out of bed on the opposite side of the glass, retrieved the crutches, and hobbled from the room, Sushi trailing down the hall close behind.

The nurses' station was vacant, and several other call buttons were blinking, indicating Wanda had been away from the desk for a while.

I was debating what to do next, when Sushi trotted down

the hallway and stopped in front of the supply room. She looked back at me, and gave two sharp barks that somehow sounded like, "*Hey! You!*"

I lurched my way to her.

With some difficulty I opened the door, a sign reading STAFF ONLY, and Sushi trotted in ahead of me.

The room, about the size of mine, contained a half dozen or so stand-alone six-foot-high metal storage units, whose shelves held a vast assortment of medical supplies, the units creating a kind of maze.

Sushi led me through a passageway into an area in the back that had a sink, coffeemaker, and a small counter refrigerator.

Seated in the corner on the cold tile floor was Wanda, her back against the wall, eyes staring at me, but not seeing. The expression on her dead face was every bit as put-upon as when she'd been living.

Mother's Trash 'n' Treasures Tip

Before attending a sale, make sure you understand what types of payment are accepted (cash, check, debit card, credit card). I learned a hard lesson by going to a cash-only sale, seeing a signed, authentic Margaret Keane print of an urchin girl, and not having enough dough. Was that an eye opener!

Chapter Eight

Shady Deal at Sunny Meadow

With Mother and Sushi both ensconced at Sunny Meadow, I had the house to myself this evening. And, boy, did I ever go wild!

For supper I heated up some tomato soup and made a grilled cheese sandwich. Afterward, I cleaned the kitchen, did a little laundry, answered a few e-mails, then checked out some Internet clothing sites. Bored with that, I turned on the TV and surfed the cable channels for a movie to watch.

I landed on TCM, which was showing Hitchcock's *Rear Window*, coming in on the part where Raymond Burr was trying to kill a wheelchair-bound Jimmy Stewart. Mother always refused to watch that movie, because she was disturbed by seeing Perry Mason behave so badly.

I turned off the TV and called Mother.

"Everything's fine, dear," she assured me. "Sushi is quite adept at eluding the staff. And I'm about to retire for the night."

In other words, don't call again.

"Okay," I said. "I'll see you tomorrow morning about eight. Nighty-night."

"Nighty-night, dear."

Feeling somewhat better, I went to bed.

But I couldn't sleep.

Vivian Borne could be formidable when faced with an adversary—if all her working parts were, you know . . . working. But an incapacitated Vivian Borne would be vulnerable, even with a feisty Sushi at her side. I growled at myself, since Soosh wasn't there to do it for me—I should have made Mother come home.

At some point I finally dozed off, and then—after what seemed like only a few minutes—was startled awake by my cell phone. The bedside clock read five in the morning. Had there been a disaster? A tragedy?

For once, I was relieved to hear Mother's voice.

"Dear," she began, "sorry to call so early, but I wonder if you could get here sooner than eight a.m."

"Well . . . sure. Everything all right?"

"I am fine and well on the mend. But there *has* been an incident."

"Define incident."

"Something out of the ordinary."

"I didn't really mean *define* it—I mean, what *happened*?"

"I'll fill you in when I see you," she said, and ended the call.

Mother was just making sure I'd rush to her side. But I thought I knew what the incident was: Sushi had been discovered and Mother had been asked to leave.

I took a quick shower, threw on some J Brand tan jeans and a Joie white eyelet blouse, slipped on Rag and Bone black flats, then went downstairs, where I microwaved a cup of last night's Dunkin' Donuts Caramel coffee, tossed a handful of Kellogg's Froot Loops into my mouth, grabbed my Coach yellow bag, and went out the door into the crack of dawn.

(**Mother to Brandy:** *Dear, you're going overboard with all of the brand names, which slows down the narrative and isn't that important.*)

(**Brandy to Mother:** *If I'm not specific, the readers will dress me themselves in their minds and I might not like what they put on me. Also, I could end up drinking Starbucks coffee, which is too strong, and eating Bran Flakes, which is just* blah.)

(**Note to Brandy from Editor:** *I think your mother's suggestion has merit.*)

Oh, *fine*. I took a quick shower, threw on some jeans and a blouse, slipped on flats, then went downstairs, where I microwaved a cup of last night's coffee, tossed a handful of cereal into my mouth, grabbed my bag, and went out the door into the crack of dawn. Everybody happy?

My conjecture about the "incident" suddenly changed when I arrived at Sunny Meadow and saw Sheriff Rudder's patrol car parked at the front entrance.

I knew the vehicle was his because of the little mark on the back bumper Mother had once-upon-a-time sneakily made with indelible black ink so she would always know it was him and not a deputy.

(**Mother to Brandy:** *I did no such thing. The mark was already on his car.*)

(**Brandy to Mother:** *I was, like, with you at the time!*)

(**Note to Brandy and Vivian from Editor:** *Ladies, if you insist upon continuing this squabbling, I'm going to pull the plug on your entire series.*)

(**Note to Editor from Vivian:** *Yes, ma'am.*)

Further evidence that something serious had happened was the paramedic's van, lights flashing, parked somewhat askew, and the coroner's black sedan.

I parked, then hurried into the building.

Stepping off the elevator onto the second floor, I was immediately met by a disheveled Mr. Burnett, who must have thrown on yesterday's clothes (no brand names— you're on your own) after being rousted from bed.

"Your mother is in her room," he said tersely. "And so is that *dog*."

"Thank you," I said pleasantly, sidestepped him, and moved on.

"And they're supposed to stay *in* there!" he called to my back. "Sheriff's orders!"

That didn't seem to require a response.

Outside the supply room stood Rudder, having a confab with two young male paramedics, and the coroner, a middle-aged, short, bespectacled bald man. His name was Hector, not that it matters, as this is his only appearance in the story.

As I neared, the men stopped talking; the sheriff's narrowed eyes followed me in wide-open suspicion as I continued on toward Mother's room.

She was in the recliner, feet up, dressed (feel free to put clothes on her, just make sure they're periwinkle), hair fixed, makeup applied, and ready for whatever new adventures the day might bring.

Sushi, on her lap, jumped down and ran to me. I picked the little darling up, got some eager licks to the face, then sat on the edge of the bed, wiping the moisture off with a sleeve.

"Well?" I asked her.

As matter-of-fact as a weather report, Mother told me how she had called for Wanda about a quarter to three in the morning and—when the nurse didn't come—used the crutches to go and search for her. Sushi had led Mother to the supply room where she found a lifeless Wanda.

I said, "Do we know the cause of death?"

"Drug overdose," Mother said. "I overheard the paramedics tell Sheriff Rudder that if they'd gotten to her sooner, she might have been saved by an injection of epinephrine."

"What about the time she died?"

"I heard Hector say between midnight and two," Mother said. "But that's all I got before being banished to this room. You'd think that man would have learned by now what a help I can be."

That man being Sheriff Rudder. As for Hector, he has now officially disappeared from this narrative.

"An accidental overdose, maybe," I said.

"Or something more sinister."

I frowned. "Any reason for that opinion, besides a thirst for murder?"

"I am no vampire, dear, just a good citizen and a candidate for sheriff. My belief derives from a simple fact—Wanda was the author of my anonymous note."

"However could you know that?"

Mother's smile was a little smug. "You will not be shocked to learn that I did a touch of snooping at the nurses' station while waiting for help to arrive. And what do you think I found?"

"Please don't make me guess."

"A report with the late Wanda's handwriting. And while *my* note was printed in all caps, there were enough similar examples in that report to prove to my satisfaction that Wanda was my wanna-be informer." Mother stroked her chin. "There's just one problem with that, however. . . . I also saw the staff's time sheet for this week, and Wanda's afternoon break yesterday was at four, yet I was due to meet her at three."

I shrugged. "Maybe she wanted to make sure you had time to get to the garden, you know, because of the wheelchair."

"But if I'd been on time," Mother said, almost crossly, "I might not have waited that long to receive her!"

I added a thought. "Maybe she wrote the note for someone else who planned to meet you."

"Perhaps."

I snapped my fingers. "Might be she was giving herself an alibi! Possible she didn't intend to meet you at all—just wanted to send you down a steep hill in a sabotaged wheelchair!"

We fell silent for a moment.

Then Mother said, "Dear, I'm afraid I owe you an apology."

Wow. I could count her apologies to me, over the years, on one hand. With fingers left to wiggle.

"You were correct about leaving Sushi with your poor, helpless mater," she said. "As things transpired, I did need her protection."

"Spill."

"I had two visitors in the night," Mother explained, leaning toward me conspiratorially. "The first was Mr. Fillmore, who came around looking for a little . . . shall we say, *faire l'amour*."

I held a hand up like a traffic cop, wishing I also had a whistle. "Don't want to hear about it. Not pertinent."

"Nothing happened, dear—I might have been *re*-clined, but I wasn't *in*-clined—and Sushi dispatched him, toot sweet. No, it was my second visitor who put me in peril. He—or she—came close enough to do me harm before I awoke and yelled, startling him and alerting Sushi, who tried to take chase, but the door closed, preventing that. Luckily, the only casualty was Gabby Hayes, who got knocked off the nightstand, and will need a new frame and glass."

"Well, that settles it," I said firmly. "You're coming home."

"No argument," Mother said. "Besides, I heard talk of a full investigation, not just of Wanda's death, but all standards and practices of Sunny Meadow. And once the regulators descend, I'll have very little access to further information."

A knock on the door announced Sheriff Rudder, who strode in with his slightly sideways gait. While his tan shirt and khaki-colored slacks looked fresh enough, he himself did not, bags beneath his eyes packed and ready for retirement.

"Vivian, Brandy," Rudder said with curt nods.

He found a chair and planted himself next to the seated Mother, who was reclined if not inclined; I remained on the bed, holding an uncharacteristically neutral Sushi, who neither liked nor disliked the man.

"Okay," he said. "What's your story, Vivian?"

Mother gave a truncated version of what she had told me (omitting her two night visitors), very straightforward with no dramatic flourishes—I knew she was eager to get to her own questions.

"Overdose, was it?" Mother asked Rudder.

"I'm not at liberty to say," he replied.

I said, "She overheard the paramedics."

The sheriff sighed (as I said, many who encounter Mother do). "All right, that *is* the suspected cause," he admitted.

"Death between midnight and two?" Mother asked.

"I'm not at liberty to speak to that, either."

"She overheard the coroner," I commented.

Rudder smirked. "Then you know everything I do."

"Perhaps more," Mother said with a pixie smile. Pixie smiles are not terribly becoming to women over sixty. They probably aren't becoming on pixies over sixty, either.

The sheriff cocked his head. "I understand you had a problem with your wheelchair yesterday afternoon."

Mother waved a hand. "A mere bagatelle."

"Ah-huh. Well, Vivian, I want you to leave this facility before there are any *more* bag-a-whats-its. *Today*."

Mother un-reclined the chair, then sat forward. "I'll make you a deal, Sheriff. . . . I'll leave by sundown, first stage out, *if* I can sit in during your interrogation of the staff. You *are* going to round them up now, aren't you?"

Insert sheriff sighing here. ". . . Yes."

She raised an eyebrow. "Well?"

He studied her. Something happened in his chest that was halfway between a grunt and a laugh. "All right," he said.

Really? That was unusual.

"And I get to ask a few questions," Mother pushed.

"One question."

"One question that can have two parts. And Brandy and Sushi get to come, too."

"No questions from Brandy," Rudder said.

I didn't know why Mother wanted me there, but Sushi might have been able to sniff out and identify their second visitor last night.

I assured Rudder, "Neither Sushi nor I will ask any questions with any parts."

His lips formed a thin line for a moment. "Okay, but Vivian has to *verbally* promise to leave here today."

The sheriff had once fallen for Mother's nodding-only ploy, which she later attributed to a condition called "essential head tremor."

Mother verbally promised.

Soon we three had gathered in a cheerfully decorated room used for family birthday parties and reunions—polished wood floor, pale yellow walls, hanging floral pictures, and a bank of windows that offered a picturesque view of the countryside. The beige sofa with end tables and matching lamps, kitchenette, and large oval-shaped modern oak dining table with six chairs made for a welcoming area.

Rudder sat at one end of the table, Mother at the other,

and the first interviewee, Mr. Burnett, was between them, his back to the door. I was on the couch, with Sushi on my lap, and she was having no reaction to the manager; but the scent of aftershave wafted toward me, which I hadn't recalled smelling on him before. I didn't even know they still sold Hai Karate.

The interview got off to a bumpy start.

"What's *she* doing here?" Burnett demanded, glaring at Mother.

"I'm giving Mrs. Borne the opportunity to see how I conduct my interviews," Rudder replied. "She may be our next sheriff, after all."

That pleased Mother, and she smiled and nodded regally.

"Heaven help us," Burnett muttered.

Rudder said, "We'll keep this informal, Mr. Burnett." Which meant no recording device; but the sheriff did produce a little pad and pen. "And as brief as possible."

"Thank you," the manager said. "I have a lot to do, in the aftermath of this tragedy, as you might imagine."

"When was the last time you saw Wanda Mercer?" the sheriff asked.

Burnett put a hand to his chin. "Well, let me think. . . . A little before six yesterday evening, I believe. I stopped up on the second floor to make sure everything was all right before I left."

"How did she seem?"

Burnett shrugged. "Fine."

"Not upset?"

"Didn't appear to be. But I did see her talking, outside, with our janitor, Blake Ferrell, about four o'clock. I was in with Mrs. Borne after Joan had examined her and just happened to glance out the window."

"Were they arguing?"

He made a dismissive gesture. "I just caught a glimpse

of them. I don't keep track of my staff's relationships. There's no antifraternization policy. My only interest in my people is that they're doing their jobs properly."

And cheaply.

The sheriff asked, "Did you know if Wanda was taking a painkiller—prescribed, I mean?"

"Not that I was aware of."

"Did you suspect she might be on one?"

"No. Not that I'd have any reason to."

"Tell me about your narcotics here."

Burnett's voice turned defensive. "What do you mean? We take the standard precautions."

"Be specific, sir. Who's allowed to handle the pills? Who keeps track of them? What checks and balances are in place to keep controlled substances from being misused?"

Burnett's sigh came all the way up from his toes. "Only Joan and Wanda are . . . were . . . allowed to handle *all* medications. Joan dispenses them. Wanda would take them around to the patients. Joan compiles a weekly report of what is used and what is not, which I sign and send to regulators."

Mother asked, "What do you do with medication that is not used?"

Uh-oh. That was her one question and it wasn't a two-parter.

Mother, realizing her blunder, added quickly, "And how often do you do what it is that you do with them?"

Huh?

Burnett's eyes shifted to her. "Unused medication is destroyed, since we can't get a refund from the supplier for it. And that happens quite often . . . when a doctor changes a patient's medication, or the patient is released before taking it all—you see, we aren't allowed to send medication home with them. And, naturally, when someone passes away and no longer needs it, disposal is automatic."

Rudder asked, "How is the medication disposed of?"

Burnett's eyes bounced back to the sheriff. "Nothing elaborate, I assure you. Frankly, usually . . . the toilet is involved."

When Mother and Rudder exchanged surprised looks, the manager rushed to add, "Always with two people present. Usually Joan and Wanda, but sometimes one of them and myself. Of course we keep records of every pill that we, er . . . flush."

Not much of a check and balance, if the two people at any given time had mischief on their minds.

Burnett sat forward, both arms on the table. "Look, Sheriff, we're doing the best we can here, hampered by increasing regulations, and being understaffed—most of the employees work long hours, often double shifts. Is there room for improvement? Of course! When isn't there?"

"Improvements," Rudder said dryly, "like replacing your out-of-commission security cam system?"

Burnett swallowed. "Our budget just hasn't allowed."

"Is the staff ever tested for drug use?" Rudder asked.

"Since it's not required in this state, no."

"You have your own pharmacy here?"

Burnett sat back, folding his arms against his chest. "No. We're not a large enough facility, nor associated with a hospital that does have its own supply. Our medications come from LTCs—Long Term Care pharmacies—that deliver our orders on a daily basis. There are two major LTCs, but we can't afford to pay for their medications, which are actually higher than most local retail pharmacies. So we use one of the smaller outfits that offer cheaper products."

And if those pills were inferior, that might account for Mrs. Goldstein's claim that her pain pills hadn't been effective.

Mother ignored her one-question rule, but kept up the

two-part aspect. "What is your policy on hiring ex-cons, Mr. Burnett? And do you have any employed here?"

Rudder must have liked the questions—both parts—because he didn't even give Mother a reproving glance.

But the manager looked at her coolly. "My policy is not to hire them. And as far as I know, no one on my staff is an ex-convict."

Rudder jumped back in. "Then you didn't know your janitor, Blake Ferrell, has a record?"

"Certainly not! I ask for that information on the employment form, and he marked 'no.'"

Rudder's frown seemed skeptical. "And you didn't bother to check him out?"

"Mr. Ferrell came with a good reference from someone I know and trust, so no, I *didn't* check it out. We are a small, private facility in a small town, as you may have noticed."

The manager's defensiveness waved a red flag.

Rudder's next question came from left field: "What were your movements the morning of the explosion, Mr. Burnett?"

The man unfolded his arms. "What? I thought we were done with that."

Mother sat forward, probably thinking the same thing I was: *Why was the sheriff revisiting the accident? Unless he believed it* wasn't *an accident, after all.*

Rudder waited for an answer.

"To my best recollection," Burnett said, voice softer now, "I was in my office all morning, except to use the bathroom and get a cup of coffee from the staff lounge."

Mother broke in. "Perhaps you've forgotten the argument you had with Harriet."

Burnett glared at her. "Who told you *that*?"

Rudder asked sharply, "Is it true?"

". . . Yes. Yes, I did pay Harriet a visit. I'd forgotten. It was a big nothing."

"At what time?" Rudder asked.

"About nine or so. You can check with . . . oh, no, you can't. I was going to say Wanda. She saw me. She was making her rounds of the apartments with morning medication, which is from eight to nine."

"Why did you pay Mrs. Douglas a visit?"

"I wanted to check Harriet's smoke alarm to make sure she hadn't removed the batteries."

Rudder's frown was thoughtful, not accusative. "Because you knew she smoked inside around her tank?"

Burnett sighed. "I did *not* know. Not for certain. But I suspected as much. And I found that the batteries *had* been removed." He paused, then went on. "But there was no argument, not really. I may have raised my voice a little when I made it clear she would have to leave Sunny Meadow if that happened again."

"Thank you, Mr. Burnett," Rudder said. "I believe that's all for the time being. Would you please ask Joan Lindle to come in?"

The manager stood. "I'll fetch her."

After the door closed, the sheriff looked sideways at Mother. "Holding out on me, Vivian?"

"I'd say you were holding out on *me*, Sheriff," she responded archly, "regarding Mr. Ferrell's police record. As for the argument between Burnett and Harriet . . . I only heard about it yesterday morning from Mrs. Goldstein. Now what *gives*?"

Rudder studied her. "Let's just say I have a reason to revisit the explosion."

"That's all you're going to say?"

"Yep."

She folded her arms. "Then perhaps I won't share with

you what I know about Harriet's reputation as a trouble-maker and whistle-blower at this oh so fine facility."

But she just had, hadn't she?

A knock came at the door. The head nurse, her working garb hanging loose on her thin figure, entered.

Rudder stood in a gentlemanly fashion.

"Thank you for coming," he said, and waved Joan to the chair Burnett had just vacated.

Only when she'd settled did he sit.

Mother and I got a glance from the nurse, but no verbal reaction to our presence. Sushi, on my lap, remained calm.

Joan said, "There's no one on the floor except Mr. Burnett, so if there's an emergency, I'll have to leave."

"Understood," Rudder said. "When was the last time you saw Nurse Mercer yesterday?"

"Just before I went off-duty at seven."

The sheriff jotted a note on his little pad.

"And how did she seem?" he asked.

Joan hesitated before answering. "I think Wanda had been crying."

"Do you know why?"

"I didn't pry. I figured if she wanted me to know, she'd tell me."

As he had with Burnett, Rudder asked Joan if she had any knowledge, or suspicion, that Wanda had been taking a controlled substance, prescribed or otherwise.

"I did not," the nurse replied pointedly. "And if Wanda had been taking what you term 'otherwise,' she certainly didn't get it from here. I keep a very tight rein on all controlled substances." Her eyes went to Mother. "For example, I know that Mrs. Borne refused pain medication yesterday morning, and the pills were returned to the dispensary and duly recorded."

Mother flinched a little, which I guessed was a reaction to a trap not sprung.

The nurse continued, eyes back on Rudder. "The person you want to talk to about Wanda is Blake Ferrell. He knows her better than anyone. They were something of . . . an item."

Mother asked, "Didn't you take Harriet a new oxygen tank the morning of the accident? And wasn't that Wanda's job?"

Joan asked Rudder, "Do I have to answer that? What official standing does this person have?"

"None," Rudder admitted. "And if you prefer, I could ask."

She drew a breath in, let it out, and said to the sheriff, "Yes, I took Harriet a new tank. She'd let her old one run out completely, and Wanda was busy organizing the medication cart. Hardly an unusual circumstance."

"What time was this?" Rudder asked.

"Around seven-thirty. It took me about five minutes to set the tank up, and then I left with the used one. Look, I thought you wanted to know about Wanda."

"I do."

"Then please stop wasting my time," the nurse snapped. "Ask Blake—I told you before: he and Wanda were intimate. And frankly, I made a point of staying out of their drama."

Rudder thought about that, then smiled faintly. "Thank you, Nurse Lindle. Would you mind finding Mr. Ferrell for me?"

Indicating with a bob of her head, she said, "He's out in the hall."

The nurse pushed back her chair, its legs screeching on the wooden floor.

Mother had no time to confab with Rudder before the door reopened and Ferrell entered, wearing a plaid shirt, blue jeans, sneakers. His face seemed drawn, troubled.

Sushi immediately had a reaction to the janitor, perking

her ears, twitching her nose. *Was he last night's mysterious intruder?* Or was her interest due to the smell coming from the fast-food sack he held in one hand?

"I hope," Rudder said cordially, "I'm not taking you away from your duties."

"It's my lunch break," Blake replied. "Would it be all right if I ate while we talk?"

"No problem," Rudder said.

Awesome!

Rudder gestured to the open chair. "Have a seat."

The janitor did, placing the sack on the table.

"You must be upset about Miss Mercer," Rudder said. "I understand you two were dating."

Blake nodded, then dipped a hand into the sack and withdrew a french fry, which he popped into his mouth. Sorrow apparently had not dulled his need for fuel.

"Was the relationship serious?"

The janitor chewed, then swallowed. "Was at first. She moved into my apartment downtown for a while, several years ago . . . but, well, we fought a lot and Wanda thought she'd be better off in her own place. After that, it was better, but we've always had kinda an on-again-off-again thing."

"I see. What about yesterday—was it on or off?"

"On, I guess, till her break at four. That's when we went outside and I told her we were through for good. I was just fed up with her moods."

"How did she take it?"

Blake shrugged. "She yelled a little, but, then, she always does. Did. Not any different than in the past."

"But in the past," Rudder said, "you'd never said you were through for good?"

"I guess."

"And that was the last time yesterday that you saw her?"

The janitor nodded, his hand going back into the sack for another fry.

"Mr. Ferrell, have you heard that the cause of Miss Mercer's death was an overdose?"

"I heard."

"Do you know if Wanda was taking any pain medication?"

"She was using something," Blake said with a shrug. "For her back, she said, from lifting patients in and out of beds."

"Do you know where she got the pills?"

Another shrug. "I assumed they were prescribed by a doctor."

"Do you think she could have taken an accidental overdose?"

He paused mid-fry before answering. "That was my first thought. See, whatever she was using didn't seem to be doing her much good, and she would take more and more, so, yeah, it could've been accidental."

"Could it have been intentional?"

The janitor's body stiffened. "What, suicide? Hell, I hope not. Wouldn't want *that* on my conscience."

Assuming he had one.

Mother raised her hand as if sitting in back, in school. "I'd like to ask the young man something, if he doesn't mind."

Blake looked her way, chewing. "Go for it."

"What was your stint in the county jail for? And how long were you incarcerated there?"

Mother's two-parter seemed to blindside him, and he stammered, "I, uh . . . I, uh . . ."

"Come, come now," Mother cajoled. "It's nothing to be ashamed of—I've spent time in the ol' hoosegow myself. Just ask the sheriff."

Rudder affirmed that. "She's right. You're not the only ex-con here, Mr. Ferrell."

The sheriff was omitting the fact that Mother's record had been expunged.

Blake shifted in his chair. "Okay. Six months for theft."

Mother kept going. "Did Mr. Burnett know about your record when he hired you? Or did you lie on your application?"

Rudder seemed not to care that Mother had taken over the interview.

"I mean, yeah, I lied on my application. So what? Sometimes you have to, to get anywhere. Anyway, I could tell Burnett was desperate to fill the job and probably wouldn't check."

"Now then, dear," Mother went on, "I want you to think back to the morning of the explosion."

Rudder was actually leaning back in his chair, arms folded, smiling gently.

The janitor frowned. ". . . Okay."

"What time did you collect the trash from the apartment of Mrs. Douglas?"

Mother no longer saw a necessity now for a two-part question.

Blake frowned. "Well, I don't know *exactly*. Sometime between ten and eleven. I used to do the apartments from nine to ten, but changed it, 'cause Wanda would be finishing her route just as I was starting, and she always wanted to talk, and I didn't want to get in bad with Burnett."

Mother pressed on. "Was Harriet smoking when you went in that morning?"

"No. If the biddy ever took that stupid risk, she was smart enough to wait till everyone made their rounds."

"Did you notice anything out-of-the ordinary that morning?"

"Like what?"

"Oh, any little thing."

"No." Then: "Oh. Well."

Mother leaned forward. "Yes?"

"Uh, I saw you"—he craned his neck my way—"and her, going around getting stuff for some sale or something. That was different."

Was he being facetious?

Disappointed, Mother sat back with a sigh. "Yes, thank you, young man. That's all."

Rudder stood. "You can go."

The janitor picked up the sack and rose. At the door, he paused, then turned. "Mrs. Borne, I knew that wheelchair shouldn'ta been used, because the screws on the brakes were bad—that's why it was in storage. Glad you didn't get yourself hurt."

And he left.

Mother and I stared at each other.

Had Burnett given her the faulty wheelchair on purpose? Had he asked Wanda to write the note, putting Mother's "accident" in motion?

Mother turned her attention to Rudder. "Now, Sheriff, you're going to tell me what you know that's made you revisit the explosion . . . otherwise you'll get no more information from me."

Rudder gave her no resistance. "The oxygen tank had indeed been tampered with."

Mother gasped. "How?"

"Now, that information I can't share at the moment."

"But . . . you're sure?" Mother asked.

"Confirmed by the manufacturer," he replied.

I had walked over with Sushi in my arms. "The manufacturer *could* be covering for a defective product."

Rudder shook his head. "The tampering was corroborated by an investigator at the DCI."

"So it *was* murder," Mother exclaimed, a little too gleefully. "I *knew* it! Come, Brandy, help me with my crutches."

"Time to get out of Dodge?" I asked.

"Yes, and for once we're beating the sheriff's time limit!"

And I'll be darned if Rudder wasn't smiling as we went.

A *Trash 'n' Treasures Tip*

Wear comfy shoes, and carry a cross-body purse to free up your hands. A bodysuit beneath your outfit will allow you to try on clothes discreetly if there are no dressing rooms. Mother goes with a friend who's her size and makes the friend try the items on.

Chapter Nine

Hang 'em High

Now that Mother was home, running the shop became impossible, so we enlisted Joe Lange, whose own mother was happy to get her admittedly eccentric son out of the house.

La Diva Borne wasted no time in having her casts removed and replaced with special medical shoes—open-toed with Velcro straps that stopped at her ankle—which enabled her to get around with the use of a cane.

She also was quick to corral me into the library/music/TV/incident room, on a sunny spring morning that offered so many better options.

I, the pupil, once again sat on the piano bench, while schoolmarm Mother stood at the antique wooden board, leaning on the cane with one hand, a piece of white chalk in the other.

Sushi had found a puddle of sunshine on the Persian carpet to curl up in.

"Dear," Mother was saying ecstatically, "I don't believe there's *ever* been a time when *both* sides of the board were required to do full justice to *two* murders."

"We know Harriet was murdered," I pointed out, "but not necessarily Wanda."

"Oh, but she was, dear."

"How can you know that?"

"Let's say I strongly suspect it," Mother replied patiently, as if I were the slowest child in class.

"And why is that?"

"Because last night—or I should say in the wee morning hours—when I went to the nurses' station to find the late Wanda Mercer, I spied an empty cup from a fast-food restaurant. Someone had thoughtfully brought Wanda coffee, which almost certainly was spiked with the opiate overdose. Possibly just to knock her out, but her own drug usage combined with the Mickey Finn proved unfortunately fatal. Or, more likely, the intention was to get rid of her for what she knew."

"The 'someone,' who did this, you assume, is the same someone who entered your room after the spurned Mr. Fillmore took his leave?"

Mother nodded. "I think he—or she—returned at a quarter to three to make sure Wanda was out of commission, then planned to harm me, but was chased off by my spirited yelling, and the unexpected appearance of our charming yapping dog. And he didn't have time—or simply forgot—to retrieve the cup."

"Why didn't you mention this to Rudder?"

She made a face. "You can *bet* he's already having that cup tested, yet he didn't mention it to *me*. The sneak! Why should I share anything with *him*?"

Mother doesn't just hold a grudge, she caresses and nurtures them.

She swiveled to the board. "Now! Let's start with Harriet." And she began to write.

When Mother had finished, a back and forth discussion began between us (which I'll spare you) to correct any dif-

ferences in our recollections, mostly regarding the suspect's Time of Last Contact (TOLC) with the woman. The
final product looked like this:

HARRIET DOUGLAS SUSPECT LIST

Name	Opportunity	TOLC	Motive
Joan Lindle	Yes	7:15–7:30am	?
Wanda Mercer	Yes	8am–9am	?
George Burnett	Yes	9:15am–9:30am	?
Blake Ferrell	Yes	10am–11am	?

"Not too promising," I said from the piano bench.

Mother sighed and studied the board. "I'm afraid
you're right, dear. A mere four suspects, one of whom is
deceased already, making her at best an accomplice. They
all had an opportunity to tamper with Harriet's tank. I
wish I knew exactly what had been done to it . . . but my
best conjecture is that the mechanism was adjusted . . . or
one might say maladjusted . . . in order to cause a slow
leak and a buildup of oxygen in the room."

"That would allow the killer to leave and be elsewhere
when the explosion came later."

"Precisely."

I frowned. "With Rudder playing his cards close to the
vest, we're guessing. Don't you have *any* snitches in the
sheriff's department?"

Mother never used money to coerce her stoolies, which
were usually women. She would exploit their weaknesses
by offering them small parts in her plays, or Godiva
chocolates, or autographed photos of pet TV or movie star
personalities of theirs, the latter usually forged by her. ("I
said they were *signed* photos, dear, and they are.")

Mother turned to face me. "I'm afraid the sheriff's-
department well has gone dry. Of course, when *I'm* sher-

iff, I'll make sure any potential leaks are plugged! But till then, there's a new dispatcher to cultivate, but I have yet to meet her."

"Whatever sabotage was done to that tank," I said, "it had to be fast, and without Harriet noticing."

"That's why Joan is my pick," Mother said, tapping the woman's name on the board. "She set up the tank, and her fiddling with it would seem normal."

"But what would her motive be? Actually, what would *any* of their motives be? What kind of dirt could Harriet have had on any of them?"

Mother turned back to the board. "Well, let's see . . . Joan could have been pilfering the pills—Wanda, too. And Harriet has already caused Mr. Burnett scads of grief. Who knows what else she had in store for him?"

"And Blake Ferrell?"

She tapped his name on the board. "Harriet could have found out our friendly neighborhood janitor had a police record, and threatened to tell Burnett."

I was nodding. "Or, more likely—since I don't think Burnett would really have cared—that Blake was in on the pill pilfering."

"Very astute," Mother said, turning toward me. "The young man certainly could be a conduit for selling the drugs, having connections from his stint in jail."

"Don't forget the political intrigue and soap opera silliness that can be part of any workplace. We already know Blake and Wanda had an on-again-off-again affair. Maybe Joan was part of that mix—or even Burnett. Or other staffers who aren't even on our radar."

We fell silent.

Then I mused, "Killing Harriet was pretty easy, as murders go, for either a man or woman to commit."

Mother frowned. "Dear?"

"Well, the killer didn't have to shoot her, or stab her, or

strangle her. Just jimmy the tank, and let Harriet's own bad judgment, smoking around it, define when the 'accident' happened. Like when it next rained, just letting things take their course."

Mother nodded. "Making it look like she unintentionally designed her own demise. Well-reasoned, dear. You are an increasingly worthy Watson."

I hoped she meant Watson in the Doyle stories and not in the old Basil Rathbone/Nigel Bruce movies she so adored, where Bruce somehow managed to be both a medical doctor and an utter dunce. Anyway, I wasn't Watson—I was Archie Goodwin. You'd think a woman who had been reading *Death of a Dude* as long as she had would know as much.

Mother gestured theatrically to the board. "Let's move on to Wanda, shall we?"

She flipped the board over and it conked her on the head, and I stifled a giggle. Who was Nigel Bruce now?

Wanda's suspect list looked similar to Harriet's—the only suspect missing was Wanda herself.

WANDA MERCER SUSPECT LIST

Name	Opportunity	TOLC	Motive
Blake Ferrell	yes	4pm	?
George Burnett	yes	6pm	?
Joan Lindle	yes	7pm	?

Mother said, "We can speculate that all three could have returned to Sunny Meadow around midnight on some pretense or other, and brought Wanda that special brew—probably a latte with whipped cream, which I'd noticed the woman had a fondness for."

I was nodding again. "If we stick with the stolen drugs, Wanda could have wanted out of the operation. That might account for her note to you, which, if someone knew about it, could have led to her murder."

"True. Then, what might Burnett's motive be?"

I shrugged. "He could have been involved with the rest of them. Perhaps Sunny Meadow was home to a ring of drug dealers, with Burnett as the mastermind!"

"Possible. Far-fetched, but possible."

"Or Burnett knew about the drug scheme and looked the other way. In a sick way, it would allow him to pay his staff poorly, knowing they had another income source."

"The kind of 'sick' that medication doesn't cure." Mother touched the chalk to her lower lip. "If I could find out who came into my room at a quarter to three, we'd *know* who the killer was."

Suddenly she sucked in air.

I sat forward. "What?"

"A session with *Tilda* might jar the ol' memory!" she declared.

I jumped to my feet, shaking my head furiously. "Oh, no! Oh, no!"

Matilda "Tilda" Tompkins was Serenity's resident New Age guru, who sometimes hypnotized Mother into remembering or anyway bringing into focus some important aspect of a case.

"Every time you go under," I whined, "another reincarnation of some past life of yours pops out! And what good does *that* ever do us? And it's always someone famous!"

"Not at all, dear. It's *never* anyone famous."

That was sort of true. She always turned out to be somebody *associated* with a famous figure in history.

In 44 BC, Mother had been Iras, handmaiden to Cleopatra, the Egyptian queen's asp page handler; in 1608 AD, she was Matoaka, younger sister of Pocahontas, and the real love (or so she claimed) of Captain John Smith; and in 1788, she was Myles Carter, personal attendant to King

George the Third, who convinced the monarch that any talk of revolution by the colonists was merely empty "poppycock."

"Even so," Mother was saying, "Tilda dispatches them quickly. And we've had very good results where retrieving clues and insights into our investigations are concerned."

I decided not to remind her about the trouble that the guru/hypnotist had with Helena Kowalski, Madame Curie's talkative cook who kept reappearing throughout one session, insisting that she (Mother) had given Madame Curie the idea of pasteurization.

Mother was saying, "Dear, if Tilda can help, you'll just have to put up with any of my former selves, though I'm sure in all their various carnations, they are quite charming and intelligent."

"A carnation is a flower, Mother, when it isn't evaporated milk. You mean incarnations."

"Incarnations, incantations, it's all in a day's work for Tilda Tompkins! Shall I call her, dear, or would you like to do the honors?"

"All right," I grumbled. "I'll give her a call."

As it happened, Tilda could see Mother in about an hour, between the guru's tantric sex class and a chakra session. So at the appropriate time, Mother and I arrived at the white two-story clapboard house, still in need of a fresh coat of paint, across from Serenity's cemetery.

I was curious to see who came out of the place from attending the tantric sex class, but we'd arrived too late, or else the members had slipped out the back way. They say tantric sex can last as long as five hours, and among the questions I had was what kind of people had that kind of time on their hands.

A cracked sidewalk led to a dilapidated porch with wicker chairs that had seen better days. Maybe they'd be plush, cushioned affairs in their next carnation.

Mother rang the bell.

After a few moments, the door opened with a hint of *Addams Family* creak.

Tilda was a slender forty-something with long golden-red hair and translucent skin, a scattering of youthful freckles across the bridge of her nose. She wore Bohemian attire—white blouse with voluminous sleeves, a long patchwork skirt, and Birkenstock sandals.

The guru/hypnotist bid us to enter, gesturing graciously, and we moved into a mystic shrine of soothing candles, healing crystals, and swirling mobiles of planets and stars—much of it for sale. Incense hung in the air like a fragrant curtain, if a curtain required you to stifle a cough, and from somewhere drifted the tinkling of New Age music. The room served as a living space, waiting area, and shop.

"I'm sorry, but there's no time to sit and partake of small talk," Tilda said apologetically. "My students will be showing up for the chakra class in half an hour."

That was fine with me. Because in addition to the multitude of candles, crystals, and mobiles in the room, a multitude of cats was stretched out on the couch (seat and back) and every chair and windowsill.

And they weren't just your ordinary, run-of-the-mill felines, either, but reincarnations of specific dead people—souls from the cemetery across the street, whose idea of "crossing over" was to come live with Tilda (or so she believed).

Mother and I followed the woman, who moved with ethereal, dreamy grace, back to the kitchen, off of which was a small, dark, claustrophobic room.

The single window had been shuttered, the only source of light a table lamp with a revolving shade whose cutout stars sent its own galaxy swirling on the ceiling. In addition to the small table and lamp, the room had a red-velvet

Victorian fainting couch (for Mother), a straight-backed cane chair (for Tilda), and a small stool for one guest (me).

The furniture had been slightly rearranged since our last visit, most notably the placement of the stool, which now was positioned where I could watch Tilda, instead of being directly behind her.

We all took our places.

Tilda addressed Mother. "Before beginning, I must reiterate that we have limited time, and therefore appearances of past lives are to be discouraged."

Mother, stretched out comfortably, said, "Yes, yes. I understand. I have prepared a script for you to read, which should address that problem."

From the pocket of her slacks Mother pulled out a folded piece of paper, on which she had written during our hour wait for the appointment, and handed it to Tilda.

"This is what you are to say," Mother instructed, "along with the questions you must ask me."

Tilda unfolded the paper, studied it for a moment, placed it in her lap, then reached to the little table for the long gold-chained necklace with its round, shiny disk.

My job was to record on my phone what Mother said *after* she was put into a trance. On our first visit, I had recorded the "putting into a trance" part, only when I later played it back for Mother, at home, she went under again, and I had to call Tilda to snap her out of it.

Dangling the necklace before Mother's face, Tilda started to swing it like a pendulum.

"Watch the medallion," Tilda said slowly, softly. "Consider its gentle motion. Surrender to its gentle motion. You feel relaxed . . . so very relaxed. You're getting sleepy . . . so very sleepy. Your eyelids are heavy . . . so very heavy . . . so heavy that you simply can't keep them open. I'm going to count backward from ten to one. When I say one, you will be asleep, completely, deeply asleep, and will respond to what I say. Ten . . . nine . . . eight . . ."

And the next thing I knew I was bent over Mother, my hands around her neck, hers around mine, and we were choking each other!

Tilda's voice, very far away, commanded, "Brandy, Vivian—wake up!"

We dropped our hands. I straightened, and Mother sat up.

"What happened?" we asked in unison, rubbing our respective necks.

The usually mellow Tilda was visibly rattled. "You *both* went under, after which Brandy reappeared as Pocahontas, with Vivian in Matoaka mode."

"Oh dear," Mother said.

I said "Oh" something.

"And," Tilda continued, "Pocahontas told Matoaka to keep her maize-pickin' hands off John Smith, and Matoaka said she wouldn't because he really loved *her*, and then you two got physical."

"You mean," I exclaimed, "*I* was Pocahontas in a former life!"

"I doubt that, dear," Mother huffed. "You are just highly suggestible, as some weak-willed persons tend to be. You were merely influenced by my appearance as Matoaka."

"Ladies," Tilda said, one hand rubbing her forehead like a magic lamp—a magic lamp with a headache. "I must remind you of my impending chakra class. We must start again immediately. Brandy, I would suggest repositioning yourself."

This time I moved my stool back behind Tilda, where I was out of range of that swinging necklace (in addition, I kept my thoughts focused on a pair of Jimmy Choo shoes I'd seen on Tradesy). Our hippie-ish hostess put Mother successfully under, with no other former life of hers or mine revealing itself.

The following is a playback of the recording that Mother and I listened to in the car in front of Tilda's house, twenty minutes later.

Tilda: *I wish to speak to Vivian Borne, and Vivian Borne alone. Is that understood?*

Mother: *Yes.*

Tilda: *Last week, at approximately two forty-five in the morning, someone entered your room at Sunny Meadow Manor.*

Mother: *Yes.*

Tilda: *I take you to the very moment when you awakened and became aware of his or her presence.*

Mother: *Yes.*

Tilda: *Your eyes have just opened. What do you see?*

Mother: *Someone is beside my bed.*

Tilda: *A man or woman?*

Mother: *Yes.*

Tilda: *(exasperated) Which?*

Mother: *. . . Can't tell.*

Tilda: *(going slightly off script) We will say "the intruder" for the sake of nongender specificity. What is the intruder doing?*

Mother: *Just standing there. The intruder has something in his or her hand.*

Tilda: *Is it a weapon? A knife, or gun, perhaps?*

Mother: *No. The intruder holds my photo of Gabby Hayes.*

Tilda: *Of . . . who?*

Brandy: *(whispered) Never mind.*

Mother: *Of whom.*

Tilda: *What?*

Mother: *Photo of whom. Framed. Under glass.*

Tilda: *Is the intruder preparing to hit you with it?*
Mother: *No, just holding it.*
Tilda: *Then what?*
Mother: *I yelled. Then the intruder dropped the frame and ran.*

The recording ended.

Puzzled, I asked, "Why would someone want *that* photo?"

Mother was frowning. "Well, I admit it's a lovely likeness. And signed movie star photos, when authentic, can be of quite some value. Where's Gabby now?"

"Still packed in one of the suitcases with the stuff from your room."

"Hmmmm. Let's go home, dear, shall we?"

Before long, we were seated on the Victorian needlepoint couch in the living room while Mother removed the vintage eight-by-ten glossy photo from its now glassless frame.

A sheet of white paper floated into her lap.

She picked the sheet up, and together we looked at it. Written in a strong hand, the letter of provenance read: *This photo was signed by Mr. Gabby Hayes during a Chicago publicity tour of* The Cariboo Trail *in 1950. Judd Pickett.*

Added below that, in the same hand, was written: *This now belongs to Daryl Dugan. Judd Pickett.*

Neither signature was dated.

Mother turned the letter over; the other side was as blank as her expression.

"Why would anyone want to steal this?" she wondered aloud. "Granted, the photo is worth a few hundred dollars, but nothing worth *killing* over! Even for a die-hard Gabby Hayes fan like *moi*."

"Perhaps there's a cryptic message in the note," I said archly. "Or if we hold it up to a mirror, the signature will spell something backward. Like in Nancy Drew." I was just making trouble.

"Perhaps there's an anagram in the signature," she said.

"I was just kidding, Mother."

"I knew you were."

"No, you didn't."

The landline phone in the living room rang, putting an end to the squabble. I got up to answer it.

"Joe Lange here," my friend said.

"Problem at the shop?" I asked.

"That's a negatory," he replied.

Joe always talked in military-speak.

"Good to hear," I said. "So what's up?"

"Tom McElroy from the pawnshop called at oh-fourteen-hundred asking for you. I wasn't sure if I should give him your cell number."

My pulse quickened. "Did he say what he wanted?"

"Also negatory. I told him you might stop by the shop, but I didn't know your ETA."

Estimated time of arrival.

"Thanks," I said. "I'll go see him. Over and out." Now he had me doing it.

Mother raised her eyebrows in silent query.

"Tell you on the way to the pawnshop," I said.

And I did, expecting a verbal lashing over withholding the old Judd Pickett murder and its vague connection to our two possible new ones.

But all she said was, "Interesting."

Fifteen minutes later Mother and I entered From Pawn to King, a buzzer announcing our presence. Mr. McElroy was behind the glass counter.

"Ah, Brandy," he said, "thanks for coming. And how are you, Vivian?"

Mother, beside herself with excitement, eschewed any

such pleasantries. "Did you find Judd's knife and pipe in one of the boxes?"

"Just a knife that might be his."

"May we see it?" I asked.

Mr. McElroy bent, then produced a large white folded handkerchief, which he placed on the counter. He unwrapped it, revealing a long knife with unpolished blade, iron guard, and handle of wood and brass rivets.

I pulled the police notice from my purse, set it on the counter, and Mother and I compared the description of the knife to the one in front of us.

"I believe this *is* Judd's," Mother said.

Mr. McElroy nodded. "My conclusion as well."

I asked him, "Do you have the records from the other pawnshop?"

Another nod. "In case I have to prove the origin of any of the merchandise."

"What do you have regarding this knife?" Mother asked, hopefully.

He smiled. "A Wanda Mercer signed the sale form."

Mother and I exchanged glances.

"And the address?" I asked.

"Four-hundred-ten Main Street."

An apartment just a few blocks away.

What Mother said next was unfathomable in its sheer propriety. "You need to call Sheriff Rudder and give him that knife. He should show it to Della Pickett, Judd's daughter, who works at the artists' gallery, and can confirm or deny its authenticity. Come, Brandy."

Stunned, I followed her out onto the sidewalk, where we faced each other, Mother leaning on the cane.

"What did you do that for?" I asked. "We finally have a real clue. It's not like you, being so responsible."

"Two reasons, dear," she said. "One, to show the sheriff

I'm willing to share information. And two, so he'll go to bat for us should we face a breaking-and-entering charge."

I smirked. "Into Wanda's apartment, you mean."

She raised a forefinger. "I believe it's Blake's apartment, dear. If you recall, our janitorial acquaintance said the late Miss Mercer lived there a while . . . during which time she pawned that knife. And *he* will be at work."

"What are we looking for?" I asked.

"Anything and everything," Mother answered, far too chipper for someone conducting a murder investigation or two.

(If you're wondering why I was going along so nonchalantly with the prospect of breaking and entering, it was because when—not *if*—we got caught, it would squelch Mother's bid for sheriff. Totally worth a brief stint in stir as an accessory.)

We took the car so Mother wouldn't have to walk with the cane, and quickly found another parking spot.

The apartment was over a hair salon in another Victorian building, its entrance via a glass door between the salon and an alterations shop. A mailbox just inside the musty stairwell had a faded label with *B. Ferrell*, which didn't necessarily mean the janitor still lived there. But the day's mail had already been delivered—letters and adverts propping up the lid—and a quick look confirmed that he did.

A long, narrow staircase covered with a dirty carpet stretched up, and I was concerned Mother would have trouble navigating it; but the landlord had thoughtfully added a wooden railing, and she made it up just fine with the use of her cane.

The landing above was just wide enough for us both as we stood before the apartment door.

"What if he's home?" I asked in a whisper.

"Why would he be home?" she whispered back.

"Sick, maybe?"

"He looked quite healthy when last we saw him."

"What if he comes back early from work?"

"He won't."

Mother seemed awfully sure of herself.

"Get my tools out of my bag, dear," she said.

Mother always traveled with two lock picks, kept in a special zippered compartment.

I did as I was told, willing to sacrifice my freedom to spare Mother the agony of defeat (and me from the agony of victory, in the unlikely event she won the election).

In less than a minute, Mother had worked her magic, and we passed through the door, closing it behind us.

"Remember, dear," she whispered. "We found it unlocked."

Which cut the "breaking-and-entering" charge to just entering, or trespassing—assuming the pair of women discovered where they didn't belong with lock picks on them were given the unlikely benefit of the doubt.

We were in a large rectangular living room, expensively outfitted: large black leather sectional, enormous flatscreen TV, lots of pricey electronic toys, shelves containing movies, video games, and CDs (apparently Blake wasn't into vinyl). The walls were mostly bare, except for the occasional band poster, and the room smelled of fresh paint and new carpet.

I said, not bothering to whisper, "Blake's job must pay better than he indicated."

"Well, dear, I understand that selling stolen drugs is highly profitable."

The apartment layout was box-car style, typical of those in Victorian buildings. An open door led us to another room—this one containing workout equipment. Another door at the far end took us into a bedroom.

"Let's search here," Mother said.

"Roger that," I said. That's where all *my* secrets were: my bedroom.

There were no windows here, as the building was in the middle of the block, making windows possible on the front and back ends of the place.

I turned on the overhead light.

The room had a modern three-piece bedroom set, in dark wood—bed, bedside table, and bureau. The bed was unmade, the tabletop home to a small lamp, an ashtray, pocket change, and a few white cash register receipts.

The top receipt caught my eye, and I went in for a closer look—from a fast-food restaurant for one latte, dated the day Wanda died, a time-stamp reading *11:32 p.m.* I called Mother over.

"Very good, dear," she said. "Take a picture of it."

I did so, using my cell phone. My adrenaline was pumping—always did, when we were breaking and entering.

Mother pointed to the black ashtray. "Interesting . . . spent matches, ashes, but no cigarette butts."

She brought the ashtray up to her nose and sniffed.

"I believe Mr. Ferrell has been having a relationship with that wild girl, Mary Jane," Mother said. "She does get around. . . . See what's under the bed, dear."

I got down on my knees, then pulled out a man's shoe box, which I placed on the rumpled bed.

Mother watched as I removed the lid.

Inside was a bag of weed, and a pipe with a long spiral stem and carved raised rings decorated with brass tacks.

I said, "Imagine. He knew he could pawn a knife, since it was a weapon, but not this tacky-looking thing, which was really worth a fortune."

After more pictures were taken, I replaced the box.

Mother had moved to the dresser, set her cane aside,

and was rifling through the drawers. I decided to check out the last room, which had to be the kitchen.

From the doorway I took everything in at once: the window offering a view of the alley, its shade half-pulled, a round dining table and chairs, row of oak cabinets, white refrigerator, dishwasher, and stove . . .

. . . and two tiles that had been removed from the drop-ceiling, exposing a crossbeam from which hung the body of Blake Ferrell, a tipped-over chair below him.

A Trash 'n' Treasures Tip

Never attend a white elephant sale looking for a specific treasure. Keeping an open mind will make the experience more exciting and rewarding. Without her mind wide open, Mother never would have come home with the banana telephone or the hot dog and bun toaster. And what would life at home be without them?

Chapter Ten

The Wild Hunch

My stomach was not the cast-iron thing Mother carried around with her, so I retreated to the couch in Blake Ferrell's living room, shaken and shaking, while she essayed the kitchen crime scene.

After a few minutes, she joined me on the sectional, resting her cane against the couch.

"How are you, dear?" she asked, her gaze clinical but her concern quite real.

". . . Okay."

But really I wasn't. I could never remove emotion from the equation and look clinically at death, the way she could.

"Your face is as pale as poor Ferrell's, dear. Do try to buck up."

I just looked at her.

She turned her gaze toward the door, saying, "I've called Sheriff Rudder because I thought he should come, even though we're on Tony's patch."

I nodded numbly.

She rattled on: "And there's no point bringing in the

paramedics. The young man's been dead for some time, judging by the lividity that's gathered in his legs."

I gave her another numb nod, glad my stomach didn't have anything in it right now to contribute.

Footsteps could be heard in the stairwell, coming up fast.

I stood, paused, collected myself, and crossed to the door. Opened it.

Rudder came in, alone, a little out of breath.

"Kitchen," I told him.

Without a word, the sheriff moved in that direction, and I returned to the couch.

Mother said, "I believe we can erase Wanda's side of the incident board, now that it seems apparent Blake killed her."

"Her, and probably Judd Pickett, too," I said.

"In the home invasion, yes."

"That leaves Harriet's death to account for. Could Blake have been responsible for that, too?"

"Joan is still my pick," she replied, as if she were selecting a horse to win in a race. "I don't see how Blake, or Wanda, or Mr. Bennett could have jimmied her tank with Harriet sitting right there using it." She raised a finger. "However, any of the three *could* have had access to it earlier."

"How?"

"Perhaps Blake unloaded the tank from the medical delivery truck, or Bennett delivered it to the dispensary where Wanda was getting the pill cart ready for the morning."

Rudder appeared, strode toward us, and planted himself in front of the couch.

"I've notified Chief Cassato," the sheriff said. "He'll be sending forensics."

Mother acted surprised. "Surely you don't suspect foul play? Aren't we looking at a rather physical confession from a cornered murderer?"

"Maybe. But there's no suicide note, which would be the place to *really* confess. Anyway, just being thorough."

"Most commendable," Mother said, a teacher praising a rather dense student.

Rudder looked down his nose at her. "Vivian, please tell me you didn't break in here."

"I didn't break in here," Mother replied.

Well . . . he told her to tell him that.

His gaze swerved toward me. "How about you, Brandy? Did she rope you into doing her dirty work?"

Mother put a hand on my shoulder and leaned close. "Can't you see the child has been traumatized by making this horrific discovery? Have you no shame, sir? At long last, have you no decency?"

She was doing her McCarthy Hearings bit.

Rudder just smirked skeptically at us.

Returning to her prior position, she said, "You'll want to take note of a receipt on the bedside table for a latte bought just a few hours before Wanda died."

"Anything *else*?" He seemed annoyed at receiving this gift of evidence from Vivian Borne.

"You're *welcome*," Mother said. "And beneath the bed you'll find a shoebox with Judd's stolen pipe inside. Which, by the way, you'll want to handle with care because it's priceless."

"I *know* that," Rudder snapped. "Della told me when she identified the knife."

"Ah! It *was* her father's."

Multiple footsteps echoed in the stairwell—more company coming.

Tony came through the door first, his steel gray eyes landing on Rudder, then going to Mother and me.

I gave him a little halfhearted wave.

He gave me a little halfhearted nod.

"You found the body?" he asked me, barely audible.

I nodded.

"We'll talk," he said. Then the chief's eyes returned to Rudder, who nodded toward the back of the apartment.

On Tony's heels came a two-man forensics team toting their gear, and the three moved on.

Rudder returned his attention to us.

"So," he asked, "how *did* you get in?"

"The door was unlocked," Mother replied.

Technically true—it *had* been unlocked. She'd unlocked it with her picks.

Rudder sighed. "And how did you happen to come here?"

"We didn't happen to come here," she said pleasantly. "We did it with forethought, but not malice—Blake hadn't shown up for work."

No lie there.

"You called out there and checked, did you?"

"What do *you* think?"

Thrust and parry.

The sheriff's voice drizzled sarcasm on his next question: "He didn't show up for work, and so of course you were concerned?"

"Naturally. And as it turned out, the concern was quite warranted." She cocked her head. "How *is* the investigation into improprieties at Sunny Meadow going? Specifically in the area of pharmaceuticals."

He said nothing, but he did sigh again; it sounded a little like a wheezing furnace.

Mother sat forward, her hands folded in her lap. "Sheriff, I'm disappointed. I had believed you and I had come to an understanding—a silent agreement to do each other favors."

"I *am* doing you a favor."

"What, specifically?" Mother asked.

His tiny smile was nasty, the upper lip curling like a dog about to growl. "I'm not going to check for pick marks on the lock. Now go home, you two."

I said, "But Chief Cassato said he wanted to talk to me."

"I'm sure he knows where to find you. Go *home*!"

But we didn't go home, instead driving to the shop.

Midafternoon now, we found Joe—in tan-and-green speckled desert fatigues—hard at work, boxing up items marked for the upcoming white elephant sale, cartons stacked in the foyer, ready for transport to the Serenity Food Bank, whose facility we'd be using in exchange for receiving part of the proceeds.

My friend went to the same mental health clinic as Mother and me—he was being treated for his PTSD (post-traumatic stress disorder). But every summer Joe made a habit of going off his meds, and packed up his survivalist gear to live in a cave at Wildcat Den State Park until fall (occasionally sneaking home to collect food set out by his mother). That's why we only could use him at the shop for another month or so.

"How's everything going?" I asked him.

"A-okay," he replied, standing at attention.

Joe was tall and lean, with nice features that were a tad wrong: eyes slightly off kilter, nose leaning left (though he leaned right), mouth a mite too wide, and thick, sandy, unruly hair that refused to surrender.

"Provide coordinates," he said, "and I can convey some of the boxes in my Jeep."

"Thank you, Joe," Mother said. "We could use your help when the time comes."

"Roger that." Then: "Noted police activity down the street."

I nodded. "Blake Ferrell . . . janitor at Sunny Meadow . . . took his life, apparently. Know him?"

"Negatory. But picked up some scuttlebutt about him."

"In what regard?" Mother queried.

"His connection to drugs."

I asked, "Connected how?"

"Dealer."

That was about as detailed as Joe got.

Risking a nonmilitary smile, he asked, "Would you like me to stay and take over, Brandy? Mrs. Borne? Otherwise I have gear to pick up."

Joe was already prepping for his summer cave vacation.

"No, you can go," Mother said. "Dismissed! . . . And thank you."

He nodded. "Want me to open up tomorrow at oh-nine-hundred?"

"Yes, please," she said. "I'm not sure what our mother-daughter itinerary will be as yet."

After my eccentric friend had gone, Mother moved to the stool behind the counter, where she sat, frowning.

"What is it?" I asked.

"Dear, I'm still perplexed about why Harriet gave me that photo of Gabby Hayes, and was so insistent that I keep it."

At the moment I didn't care. I was hungry.

"Maybe she was just being nice," I said, and went back to the kitchen and got the cookie dough out of the fridge, fired up the stove, and started some coffee going.

Mother continued talking as if I were still with her.

"Maybe his *name* contains a clue," she said out there, never hard to hear from a distance thanks to her stage training.

Her fingers could be heard clicking on the computer's keyboard, and I knew she was probably using one of the anagram sites.

Too impatient to wait for the oven to preheat, I put the tray of dough inside—knowing I'd probably have burnt cookie bottoms—and set the timer.

I returned to Mother. "Well?"

"Zip, zally, zilch."

She looked the actor up on Wikipedia, and when she

started to read his biography out loud, I pulled up the extra stool. Nothing jumped out from the bio, but Mr. Hayes had led a long and interesting life.

"What about his movies?" I asked. The biography mentioned Gabby had appeared in over one hundred and fifty films, but didn't list them.

Mother went to IMDb.

The oven buzzer sounded, and I hopped off the stool.

Yep, burnt bottoms. Better theirs than mine.

Her voice reached me from the other room. "I'll read them. *Don't Fence Me In, Along the Navajo Trail, The Man from Oklahoma, Under Nevada Skies, Song of Arizona, Rainbow Over Texas . . .*"

I got myself some coffee.

"*. . . Badman's Territory, Return of the Bad Men, Home in Oklahoma, Trail Street, The Untamed Breed . . .*"

I ate a cookie.

"*. . . Mojave Firebrand, The Big Bonanza, Tall in the Saddle, Tucson Raiders, The Man from Thunder River . . .*"

I had another cookie.

"*. . . Overland Mail Robbery, Death Valley Manhunt, Wagon Tracks West, Man from Cheyenne, Sons of the Pioneers . . .*"

And a third cookie.

"*. . . Hidden Valley Outlaws, Lights of Old Santa Fe, Marshal of Reno, Red River Valley,* bring me a cookie."

For a nanosecond I thought—*Bring Me a Cookie,* what an odd name for a western.

I put a few lesser burnt-bottomed cookies on a plate, poured coffee in a cup for her, and rejoined Mother.

Settling back on the stool, I said, "We'll be here for hours if you read out all of his films—what was the one mentioned in the letter of provenance?"

"*The Cariboo Trail.*"

"What's it about?"

Mother looked it up. " 'Two ranchers, played by Randolph Scott and Bill Williams, drive their cattle from Montana to Canada along the Cariboo Trail, but one night the herd is stolen from them, stranding them in the wilderness. They then try to earn money by panning for gold with the help of an old prospector, played by Gabby Hayes. But soon their gold is stolen, too.' " She nibbled on a cookie. "Admittedly, it's not among Randy Scott's finest movies, but Gabby Hayes gives one of his best performances, says here. When are you going to learn to preheat that oven?"

Ignoring her question, I said, "Maybe a map of the Cariboo Trail will tell you something."

Okay, so maybe I was just making trouble again. But that was better than Mother getting into real trouble— there could still be a murderer out there, you know.

The bell over the door tinkled, announcing a visitor, putting a temporary end to this nonsense.

Tony came in.

"Vivian, Brandy," he said, businesslike, and approached the counter.

"Hello, Chiefie," Mother chirped, using the silly nickname that always made his eyes tighten a little.

Those eyes went to me. "I'd like a private word with your daughter."

Uh-oh.

I slid off my stool. "How about some coffee? I've got a fresh pot going in the kitchen."

"Fine."

Mother, looking miffed that she hadn't been included, said, "Don't be concerned about me. . . . I'll just take a trip along the Cariboo Trail."

Tony shot her a quizzical look, then followed me.

He sat at the vintage Formica-top table, while I got us both some java (a fifties expression at a fifties table), then joined him.

"What's this about the Cariboo Trail?" he asked.

I waved a dismissive hand. "Just a silly false lead I tossed Mother to keep her occupied . . . If this is concerning how we got into Blake's apartment . . . ?"

"It isn't. I'm in no mood to be your conscience right now. And, frankly, that won't make any difference with the evidence we've found."

"Oh." I waited.

Tony took a sip of coffee, then sat back. "I want to know when Vivian is going to resume her campaigning."

I frowned at this apparent non sequitur. "You mean, when is she going to be through investigating?"

He nodded.

"Well, I think Mother is satisfied that Blake killed Judd Pickett, and Wanda, too, and then took his own life. But she's hung up—sorry, bad word choice—on who might've murdered Harriet."

"Is she." It wasn't exactly a question.

I nodded. "According to Rudder, Mrs. Douglas's oxygen tank had been tampered with, and Mother won't stop till she finds out who did it."

Tony expressed his disgust with a cross between a grunt and a growl.

"Then," he said, and sighing (lot of that going around), "you'd better call her in here."

But I didn't have to, because she'd been listening just outside the doorway.

After Mother had settled in to the chair across from Tony, he asked her, "Have you met Emma, our new dispatcher?"

What did the new dispatcher have to do with the price of coffee beans?

"Funny you should mention her," Mother replied, innocently. "I was planning on dropping by the station to get acquainted. To wish her all the best in her new endeavor."

Mother, of course, had never met Emma.

With his eyes narrowed and his smile narrower, Tony said, "Perhaps you'd like a little background on her."

"Please." Mother folded her hands primly. "Any information would be helpful in forging a friendship."

Such as, did Emma like Godiva chocolates, small parts in plays, or photos autographed by movie stars?

The chief said, "Emma is perhaps the best dispatcher we've ever had, and it's just the beginning for her. Her husband gave up an excellent job in Indiana just so she could get her start in law enforcement. Their two children were pulled out of private schools to be enrolled here, and they just bought a house with a hefty mortgage."

Those were more words than I'd ever heard Tony string together.

"How delightful," Mother said.

"Yes, and I'd hate to have to fire Emma for giving you confidential information after all the sacrifices her family has made."

Mother, instead of being offended, sat forward, eyes gleaming. "What deal are you offering me?"

Now Tony formed a sly smile the likes of which I'd never seen from him. "First—Emma. I don't want her compromised."

Holding up her hands, fingers splayed, Mother might have been surrendering, or possibly demonstrating that her fingers were not crossed. "I'll never pressure the woman for information," she stated flatly.

"Brandy," Tony said, his eyes still on Mother, "you're a witness."

I said, "I will do my best to see that Mother keeps her word." For what good it would do.

"All right," Tony said. He regarded us both. "A stun gun was used on Blake before he was hanged."

Mother's mouth dropped open—mine, too—like the trap door on a gallows.

"He was Tased?" I asked. Mother had once accidentally shot me with her Taser gun and I was paralyzed for about half an hour. Good times.

Tony shook his head. "A Taser and a stun gun are slightly different weapons. They both use an electrical current to render a person helpless, but a Taser can be activated from a distance, while a stun gun has to be held right against the person. The marks of a stun gun were found on Blake Ferrell's back."

I felt the hair on the back of my neck tingle. "So he knew and probably trusted his attacker."

"And once Blake was helpless," Mother said, her eyes slitted but glittering, "some person unknown set the stage to make a murder look like a suicide."

"Didn't it have to've been a man," I asked, "to lift Blake up high enough to . . . ?"

I shivered and Tony shrugged.

"The victim didn't weigh that much," he said. "A woman, with adrenaline going, might be capable."

"A stun gun is more of a female's weapon, isn't it?" I asked. "Something to use for close contact? Like mace?"

Tony shrugged again. "Not necessarily. Some of our male officers prefer a stun gun to a Taser. Different strokes."

For several seconds there was no sound but the *tick tock* of our Felix the Cat clock.

Then Tony stood, eyes on Mother, unblinking and hard. "Vivian, I want you to stop any investigating you're doing—or plan to do. I know such requests in the past have fallen on deaf ears, but this killer is obviously dangerous, and getting more desperate. Let Rudder and me do our jobs."

She nodded. Tony, like the sheriff, long since learned to ask Mother for a verbal agreement.

"Say it, Vivian," he said.

"I will let you and the sheriff do your jobs."

This, of course, did not really exclude her investigation from continuing, but Tony pushed no further.

He thanked us for the coffee, then left. For once I did not follow him to the door. I was trembling and afraid—don't mind telling you.

I said, "He's right, you know."

But Mother didn't reply—never a good sign, when Vivian Borne turns untalkative. Those wheels were turning. You could almost hear the *clank*.

The phone in the other room rang, and I left the table.

"Trash 'n' Treasures," I answered.

"Brandy?"

The voice was female and I recognized it. "Hello, Della. What can I do for you?"

This near closing time, I hoped whatever it was wouldn't keep me from getting home to a neglected Sushi.

Her voice sounded urgent. "I must see you and Vivian."

"When?"

"Now. It's important."

Sushi would have to wait. Or if she didn't, I would have to be prepared to clean up the mess.

"Are you at the gallery?" I asked.

"Home. I didn't work today."

I recalled she lived in Stoneybrook, the same housing development where Daryl had his home, and was about to ask for the number when she said, "But I don't want you to come here. And I don't want to meet at your shop or house."

A note of unease had crept into her voice.

"Do you know where the Cinders is?" she asked. "It's a sort of a bar on Main Street."

"I've been in there a few times."

"They won't be busy now, and way in the back are little private seating areas."

"Cool," I said. "See you there right away."

As I hung up, Mother asked, "What was that, dear?" She'd just come in from the kitchen.

I relayed the conversation.

"I wonder what could be so important," Mother said, clearly relishing the mystery of it. "And why the secrecy?"

"I guess we'll find out," I replied.

We locked up the store and left.

The Cinders, located on the first floor of another box-car-style Victorian brick building, had been in the same family for decades. The current owner was Renny, a lady in her early fifties, with a bubbly personality, long blond hair, pretty features, curvaceous figure, and a preference for leopard-print attire on loan from SCTV's Edith Prickley.

An avid collector of oddball collectibles, Renny had filled the bar with hundreds of such items, all for sale, although nothing was marked, and a customer who'd gotten a little tipsy might be seen leaving with a life-size standee of Mr. Spock, a velvet painting of Muhammad Ali, or a color-fully jacketed album of 78 rpm records by Gene Autry.

Without knowing it, or perhaps sensing a coming trend, Renny had, in her years of indiscriminate collecting, made the bar a magnet for the local hipster crowd, twenty- and thirty-somethings who hung out there.

I had been inside the establishment a few times, but this was Mother's first visit, accompanied by her eyes popping as they took in a huge dollhouse, completely furnished, and a vast collection of Elvis memorabilia, just inside the door.

Along the left wall stretched a bar along which were spaced lava lamps, providing ambiance, with seating at the counter consisting of a dozen red vinyl bucket-seat chairs, all empty at this early hour. In fact, we seemed to be the only customers.

Hugging the right wall, and nearly as long as the bar, was a shuffleboard-by-hand game, with little round tables and chairs provided for players to keep score.

The owner, behind the bar, looked up from drying a glass, and gave us a smile. "Welcome, ladies. Remember, everything's for sale . . . almost." And she winked at us.

I said, "Hi, Renny. Thought I'd show Mother your place—she's never been here before."

"Sure, kids, have a look around, and if you see anything you want, make me an offer. In the meantime, can I get you something to drink?"

I ordered a white zinfandel, and Mother requested her standard fare—a Shirley Temple—and informed our hostess that we'd be in the rear seating area.

Mother and I continued on, past a vintage sixties juke box, several eighties video game consoles, a table containing a half-finished jigsaw puzzle, a junior-size pocket pool setup, a collection of sombreros and boa feathers on a coatrack, more tables and mismatched chairs. The walls were covered with movie posters, sports memorabilia, mirrors of all kinds, framed movie and TV glossies, and everywhere were lighted roping and twinkle lights—Christmas in Pee-wee's Playhouse.

Through a hanging beaded curtain, we reached the last area, a cozy place made up of an assortment of kooky seating and side tables, arranged in little nooks of privacy, separated by fake palm trees with stuffed monkeys in their branches. We had the place to ourselves. Except for the monkeys.

I sat on a black chair shaped like a high heel (the chair, not me), and Mother settled on what had once been the

front seat of a fifties car with blue tuck-and-roll uphol-
stery.

"Well!" Mother said. "I'm certainly impressed. Everything *including* the kitsch and sink!"

"Don't get any ideas. We have enough stuff in the shop
and at home as it is."

"There's always room for Jell-O, dear," she said, nodding toward a framed magazine ad with Jack Benny hawk-
ing the stuff circa 1942.

Renny appeared with our drinks, in glasses with car-
toon characters (me, Daffy Duck; Mother, Bugs Bunny)
and placed them on the little table between us.

"We're expecting a third," I said. "Della, from the art
gallery? Would you send her back when she comes?"

"Of course. Lovely gal—she bought a Dale Evans Little
Golden Book from me, once. Enjoy your drinks." The
owner retreated to her fortress of pop memorabilia.

We sat in silence, sipping from the glasses. After fifteen
minutes, though, I became worried that Della wasn't here
yet—she had suggested the place, after all—and that maybe
something had happened to her.

I was just getting antsy when the beaded curtain parted,
revealing the woman. She wore a light blue blouse, an artsy
glass-beaded necklace, dark jeans, white tennis shoes, and
carried a tan handbag. I am omitting brand names because
(a) it irritates some people, and (b) I had no idea what they
were.

I got up and pulled over a red chair in the shape of lips,
so Della could join us.

"Something to drink?" I asked her.

"No," Della said, seated, if somewhat uncomfortably.
"I already told Renny I wasn't having anything."

"Now, then, dear," Mother said, "what was so urgent?"

Della stared at her hands in her lap. Her sigh was endless, despite Mother not having caused it. "I just don't know where to begin."

"Take your time, dear," Mother said patiently, but I could feel her tapping her foot next to me as if keeping time to "Tiger Rag."

Della took a deep breath and let it out. "Well, ever since I found out that Dad had sold that Wyatt Earp poster, I just can't get it out of my mind. Just doesn't ring true!" She paused, her eyes going to Mother. "Tilda Tompkins told me that sometimes she helps you remember details through hypnosis. I'm in her tantra sex class, you see."

I had a momentary brain freeze trying not to picture Della as one of the students.

She was saying, "This afternoon Tilda regressed me back to the morning of the day Dad died, when I last went to see him. She asked me if the Earp poster was still on the wall."

"And?" Mother asked excitedly.

"I said yes, it was there that morning. But later, when she took me back to when . . ."—her voice cracked—"to when I returned to Dad's house to identify his body, the poster was missing from its spot."

I asked, "Was the sheriff's department the first responder that night?"

"Yes. And I know what you're thinking . . . that Daryl Dugan had taken it . . . but he wasn't there—only Sheriff Rudder and the paramedics."

Mother said, "It's obvious now that Blake Ferrell took the poster along with the knife and pipe."

Della shrugged, shook her head.

"Then," I asked Mother, "how did *Daryl* end up with Wyatt?"

"There are but two possibilities," Mother said. "Mr. Ferrell either sold it to Daryl, whose desire for the antique poster was enough to make him abandon his sense of duty . . . or Ferrell was directed by the deputy to steal it for him in the first place."

I nodded, eyes narrowing, picking up on the latter theory. "With the proviso that Blake could help himself to any cash he found."

Mother raised a finger. "Then, when things went awry, Blake pressured Daryl to help get him a job at Sunny Meadow."

Della's frustration was obvious. "But how can any of that be *proved?*"

Mother said, "We have to get our hands on the letter of provenance your father wrote that came with the poster. Dollars to donuts the part that said Daryl was the new owner was forged."

I caught Mother's eyes. "We could compare it to the one that came with the picture of Gabby Hayes. *That's* authentic."

"Good heavens!" Mother exclaimed. "*That* must be why Harriet gave me the photo. *Cariboo Trail* my caboose! She somehow knew, or suspected, that Daryl was connected to Judd's murder and *knew* that was a clue."

Della raised a finger. "Keep in mind Dad's handwriting will be shakier on the poster's letter of provenance, written a year before his death."

I was nodding. "As compared to the Hayes letter, written years before."

"Still," Mother said, "any forging should be easy enough to tell."

I frowned at her. "So how do we get our hands on the poster to make a comparison? Breaking into Blake's apartment was one thing, but the home of a deputy? We could get arrested . . . or shot."

Della lifted a forefinger. "There's one thing Dad had

that Daryl wanted even more than that poster—the Smith and Wesson Model Three that Wyatt Earp used in the gunfight at the O.K. Corral."

"Do you still have it?" Mother asked excitedly.

"It's in my safe deposit box," Della replied.

"Would you trust us with it?"

"Yes. But be careful, it's loaded. My father said the weapon was fully functional, and he fired it occasionally. Said he got a charge out of shooting the same gun Wyatt used at the O.K. Corral."

"Near the corral," I said.

"Pardon?"

"Nothing."

I might have explained, but was too busy keeping my head from spinning at the thought of Mother at large with a loaded gun. But of all the weapons in the world, why did it have to be this one? A valuable antique that only an old collector nut like Judd Pickett would have dared fire?

Mother raised her Bugs Bunny glass as if in a toast. "Then I have a cunning plan."

She delivered this in her British accent, which I hoped was only due to her quoting the BBC *Blackadder* TV show. Because I had a feeling things were going to get dodgy enough without having to endure that.

A Trash 'n' Treasures Tip

Never attend a sale with a disinterested person (or even semi-disinterested) who will ruin the hunt and want to leave before you've searched every nook and cranny. Mother will abandon her best friend on the off-chance of discovering midcentury ceramic cowboy-and-horse salt and pepper shakers.

Chapter Eleven

Pistol-Packin' Mama

Mother, Sushi, and I were at the Playhouse Theater, about five or six miles out in the country, a repurposed old barn where once-upon-a-time community actors would gather and perform on a makeshift stage to the delight (and forbearance) of family and friends. Even now you could almost hear Judy Garland and Mickey Rooney calling out, "Come on, gang . . . let's put on a show and save the farm!"

Over the years, largely thanks to Mother's tenacious fund-raising, the barn had been transformed into a modern theatrical facility, with new additions and a state-of-the-art auditorium. All these years later, the only thing left of the original structure was its rooster weather vane.

Late afternoon on a Monday, the theater was dark—both in theatrical terms and illumination-wise—and Mother had let herself and her own personal Gabby Hayes–type sidekick (me) in through the side stage door with a key granted her as one of the theater's board of directors.

At the moment, she and I were in the star's dressing room, Mother seated at the makeup table, me standing behind her but leaning in; Sushi was off exploring, as she loved to do in these environs—especially the prop room with its various items and their many smells. (Sometimes the prop manager would find a mysterious bite taken out of a taxidermied animal, the little mutt unable to contain her primitive impulses.)

Right now Mother was applying latex skin to her face in order to change its contour.

"This plan is neither cunning," I said, "or workable."

"That's *nor* workable, dear," she said, frowning at me in the mirror. "And *of course* it's workable. Must you always be such a Debbie Downer?"

I'll let you be the judge. Is this cunning? Or workable?

Mother planned to pose as a male collector of western memorabilia by the name of Tex Ranger, from the great state of, yes, Texas, having contacted Deputy Dugan with an offer to trade the Earp O.K. Corral gun for the Earp for Sheriff poster. That would put the latter's letter of provenance in our possession, so we could check its authenticity against the one we had with the Gabby Hayes photo.

Might there have been an easier way to accomplish that? Possibly. Maybe even probably. But do you really think you or anyone could convince Vivian Borne of that?

It wasn't the trade aspect that concerned me—Dugan had agreed to the exchange readily enough, probably fine with ridding himself of evidence that could connect him to Blake Ferrell, and thus the death of Judd Pickett, and accomplishing that while acquiring an even more valuable western antique than the one he was giving up.

Convincing the deputy of the gun's authenticity was no problem, as he had been referred by Tex to Della Pickett, who assured him that the gun had indeed belonged to her father, and was sold to Ranger some years ago; nor was it difficult to convince Dugan of the existence of this unlikely named Tex, because Joe Lange had concocted a fake website for the collector, along with planting several glowing articles about him on the Internet.

So maybe the plan was cunning at that. But workable?

My concern was with Mother's disguise, which I imagined would wind up looking like something Inspector Clouseau might have dreamed up. What worked on stage, from the back of the house—or even the front row for that matter—seldom convinced up close and personal.

As Mother applied a fake bulbous nose, I idly commented, " 'False face must hide what the false heart doth know.' "

"*Brandy!*" she practically screamed, fake flesh hanging off her face like a melting Oz witch. "You've quoted from the Scottish play!"

"I have?" I always get my Shakespeare mixed up.

She pivoted in the chair to face me. "Do you know what you've *done?*"

I did.

Or anyway I knew what she *thought* I'd done. Quoting from *Macbeth* was bad luck for an actor, even worse than just speaking the play's forbidden name. Using lines from the Bard's masterpiece was only permissible during a rehearsal or an actual performance. And it was a really, really bad thing to do in a dressing room.

"Sorry," I said.

"Sorry indeed! You may have jinxed my meeting. You *know* what you *must* do."

I'd seen the ritual performed by others who had made such a mistake.

I went out of the dressing room door into the hall, shut the door, knocked two times, opened the door, came back in, spun around three times, spit on the floor, and said a swear word.

Mother nodded her approval of my performance, but chastised me for the swear word, which she claimed "didn't have to be *that* foul."

Hers was a mild *piss pot*, but still within the accepted parameters of curse words by theater folk when trying to dispel the *Macbeth* jinx. The real reason she disapproved of my choice of swear word was that it seemed to be an editorial comment on my part (the first syllable was *bull*).

She swiveled back to the mirror and picked up a scrap of paper. "Here . . . make yourself useful. Find me these clothes."

I took the list.

Wardrobe was next door to the prop room, and I called, "*Sushi! Wardrobe!*"

She scurried out from somewhere to join me—not because she missed me, but because Shoosh had been forever banned from wardrobe after shredding a white feather boa used in *Gypsy*, which had cost her mistresses a pretty penny.

I said, as if she could understand (and maybe she could), "We're looking for men's western clothes," and we proceeded to that section of the room.

Ten minutes later I had made a pile of clothing possibilities on the floor, an assortment of western shirts, vests, jackets, trousers, scarves, string ties, belts, hats, and boots (ones roomy enough so that La Diva Borne's recently operated-upon feet, sans the medical shoes, would be relatively comfortable). Only one item on Mother's list was not among the western wear—the padding an actress would strap around her waist to look pregnant (in Mother's case, creating a potbelly)—which I retrieved from another section.

Then I couldn't find Sushi.

I called for her. And called again. Slowly the pile of clothes began to move as if with a life of its own, and she crawled out from underneath, tangled up in a shirt, a red-and-black-and-white paisley bandana around her neck. I got Sushi loose from the shirt, but when I tried to take away the scarf, she growled, so I left it on her. Maybe *she* was Gabby Hayes. But what did that make me—Trigger?

I found a small, portable rack on which to hang the clothes, putting the boots on the shelf below, and the hats on the one above, and wheeled it out of the room, Sushi with the scarf trotting happily behind.

At the dressing room door, just as I was about to come in with the rack, Mother called out, "Just leave it, dear! Go out to the auditorium and await my entrance."

She wanted to surprise me with her new persona.

Do I really have to report my sigh?

Sushi came along with me, anticipating a game we would sometimes play among the rows of seating—mostly her hiding and me seeking. She always had to give me help via a little yip or yipe, but then by the time I got to where she was, she'd be somewhere else.

Pooped, I was ready to call it quits when the stage lights above the closed velvet curtains came on. Then the curtains parted in the middle, and Tex Ranger himself stepped through, walking confidently out to the apron of the stage and into the pool of the center light.

Tex was sporting a tan Stetson hat with a black band, wisps of silver hair peeking out from beneath, complementing the silver handlebar mustache. He wore a brown leather vest over a blue shirt, a brown belt with silver buckle, and tan slacks, the legs tucked in to the tooled leather shaft of black cowboy boots.

I had expected an over-the-top Buffalo Bob Smith or maybe Slim Pickens, but Tex's attire was both expensive-looking and tasteful.

But could his/her face pass the Noxzema close-up test?

I ascended the side steps to the stage, walked toward

Tex, and stood right next to him/her. Try as I may, I could not detect Mother anywhere behind the mask of prosthetic nose, makeup, and facial hair, all skillfully applied.

She even passed the Sushi test, the little dog, having joined us onstage, treating Mother (her own natural scent masked by all that makeup and worn-by-many theatrical clothing) as a stranger—whether friend or foe yet to be determined.

But what about Mother's voice? Earlier, she had called Dugan as Tex using Della's phone, to set up the meeting, and did it rather well, I thought. But could she be convincing in person?

Mother, as if reading my mind, launched into a dialogue; her voice lowered, but not ridiculously so, dialect southern, but not too good-old-boy.

"Ah remembah the first cattle drive of mah storied youth," she began, in an easy drawl. "How the smell of Arbuckle's coffee wafted from the chuck wagon as the campfires glowed in the night, and the doggies stirred gently in the moonlight . . ."

"Okay," I said, nodding. The doggie at my feet stirred, finally recognizing Mother. "But don't go off script at the meeting."

Mother's voice came out of the man's mouth. "Dear, I never go off script."

I had seen her go off script countless times, particularly in comedies when she got wind of what made the audience laugh. But this was no comedy.

"You ready for this?" I asked her.

In Tex's voice, she said, "Ah was born ready, little lady." Then in her own voice, she cackled, "*Vivian* Borne ready!"

I could have sworn I heard Sushi sigh.

The meeting for the trade had been set for eight o'clock this evening, at the riverfront, on a park bench next to a bronze statue of an Indian chief whose tribe had once ruled the area.

Dusk would be settling in, providing some cover for Mother, and foot traffic in the park should be minimal. Plus, seated next to Mother, Dugan wouldn't be able to study "Tex" quite as closely as he might across a table in some restaurant or other better-lit meeting place.

I had a part to play in tonight's performance as well, as did Della.

Hers was to be at her house in Stoneybrook, her home near the only entrance/exit to the housing development, where the Dugans also lived. There she would watch the deputy's comings and goings, keeping us posted via cell phone.

My role was to be stationed near the bench, in case something went wrong—exactly what I was to do in that circumstance wasn't clear—and the only hiding place available to me was inside a garbage can across from the bench along the river walkway.

At least the can had been kept fairly clean, thanks to a plastic liner, which I removed with its half-full contents and transferred in a wad to another receptacle. The space inside the now-empty can should be large enough for me to crouch within, without being seen, though the bouquet of *eau de garbage* still lingered.

The can also had the added benefit of little slits at the top that would allow me a straight-on view of the bench. Still, I was less than thrilled by my hidey-hole—I doubted Gabby Hayes or Smiley Burnette had ever been subject to such humiliation—and would stay out of the can until the last minute.

My cell sounded at seven-thirty. Della had told me that her cell ID was blocked, but I recalled the number she'd given me, and answered.

"He's on the move," she reported.

Since it was a fifteen-minute ride at best to the river-front, where parking was ample, the deputy apparently planned on beating Tex to the park, perhaps wanting time to watch Ranger roll in and run the plate number on his vehicle.

But there would be no car, ours being parked behind the shop just a few blocks away. And we'd already beaten him here.

We took our places—Mother on the bench, the antique weapon inside a wooden, red-velvet-lined box on her lap; me in the can, with the cell phone now switched off.

As the minutes dragged by, I became aware of voices, one male, one female, and through the slats saw a young couple strolling along the walkway, coming our way. As they passed by the can, a hand hovered over the top, and then I was clunked in the head by a large plastic cup, showered in ice, and sticky, syrupy soda.

After the pair moved out of earshot, I whispered harshly, "Why didn't you stop that?"

It wasn't Tex who replied. "How, dear? Do you expect me to blow my cover?"

"I don't know how! But remind me to kill you later."

"I should never have allowed you to watch those terrible Three Stooges after school. Don't you think I'm uncomfortable, too, in this getup?"

I grunted, then spotted the deputy striding across the park lawn. "Cheese it!"

The lanky but muscular Dugan was wearing civilian clothes—a yellow polo shirt and blue jeans. Tucked under one arm was the framed poster.

As he approached the bench, Tex drawled, "Mistah Dugan, thank ya'll for agreein' to meet me here. Ah do so enjoy a beautiful sunset. Ah hear Mark Twain praised these Serenity sunsets. We have lovely ones ah-selves in

Galveston, but this may rival it some. Hope y'all don't mind me not risin'—lumbago, yuh know."

She was pushing it, already embroidering the script.

"Not at all," Daryl said, and leaned the poster against the front of the bench, then sat.

"Ahh," Tex said, eyeing the framed poster, propped between them, "mind if ah have a look?"

"Go right ahead."

Tex picked it up and studied it. "Excellent. Excellent. Ah assume there's a letter of provuh-nance. . . ."

"Inside."

"Might ah remove the paper for a look?"

"Be my guest."

Tex removed the paper sealing the back of the frame, and gave the document within a close look. "Fine, fine . . . 'pears in order."

Dugan now examined his end of the trade, taking the box, extracting the gun, examining it closely, along with its letter. While this probable murderer had the gun in his hand, I could feel something cold running up and down my spine, and it wasn't discarded soda.

Returning both weapon and paper to the box, the deputy said, "I do have a few questions."

"Shoot," Tex replied affably.

But please don't.

"Why are you giving up this gun for something less valuable?"

"Why, value is in the eye of the beholduh, Mr. Dugan. There is only one Earp O.K. Corral gun, and only one campaign poster for the great man's failed sheriff run is known to exist. That's why Judd Pickett never put a monetary figure on any of his treasures. And ah value the poster more than the gun for two reasons."

"Which are?"

"One, ah don't trade in firearms anymore—not since mah store got busted into three times, and guns were all the thieves took." Another pause. "Two, the belief that this gun was used by Earp at the O.K. Corral has been questioned by some experts."

Dugan nodded. "Those who think he carried a Colt forty-five or a rifle that morning."

"Exactly." Tex sighed. "Even though reliable evidence has surfaced that he had this Smith and Wesson Model Three, the recent sale of a Colt forty-five at auction for three-hundred-thousand, claimin' to be *the* gun, continues to muddy the waters."

"I think he carried *this* gun," the deputy said.

"As did Judd Pickett."

Mother, pronouncing the *P* in Pickett with too much verve, caused half of her mustache to flap loose.

But Dugan had been gazing down at his soon-to-be possession, and Mother quickly pressed the mustache back in place.

"Then do we have a trade, mah friend?" Tex drawled.

"We do," Dugan replied, offering his hand to shake, which Tex did, perhaps pumping it with a little too much enthusiasm.

One more formality had to be completed, which was for each man to make a notation on the provenance papers that the poster now belonged to Clarence "Tex" Ranger, and the gun to Daryl R. Dugan, with their signatures. Della had taken care of emulating her father's handwriting on the gun's letter of provenance transferring ownership to Tex Ranger.

This seemed to take forever as I crouched all sticky and uncomfortable in the garbage can. *I just have to get out of the sidekick business,* I thought.

Then Tex said, "Reminds me of a trade ah once made with a Pawnee Indian. . . ."

Oh, please, Mother, *don't.*

". . . but ah imagine you're anxious to take your treasure home. Perhaps we should curtail the palaver."

Phew.

"Yes, if you don't mind," Dugan said, standing. "Can I give you a lift somewhere, or . . . ?"

"No, no. But thank ya kindly. Ah'm stayin' put till the sun sets, to see just what ol' Sam Clemens was talkin' about. If you're ever in Galveston, do stop by the shop. You might find more treasures."

I waited until the deputy had driven off and was out of sight, before extricating my sticky self from the can. I don't know whether I was more relieved to see that Mother had safely gotten away with it or just happy not to be one great big piece of garbage anymore.

"What now?" I asked.

Mother said, "Now you return to the shop, dear, but don't come back for me until you've heard from Della that our deputy friend is back home. I'll sit here and enjoy the sunset. He could always double back to check up on me, you know."

"And if he does? If he saw through your performance?"

She replied in character: "That's why ol' Tex never goes anywhere without his trusty can of mace, sugah."

I nodded and clomped off, soles of my shoes sticking to the pavement.

Reaching Trash 'n' Treasures, I went inside where Sushi seemed extra happy to see me—or maybe it was just the sugary syrup.

I was debating going upstairs to the working bathroom to clean up, and exchange my nasty clothes for some vintage ones from our stock, when my cell sounded.

"He's back," Della said, then asked, "You'll call me after you compare the letters?"

"Yes. But give us some time. We'll be going back to our house to examine them."

"I'll be waiting."

I scooped Sushi up, locked the shop's front door, and went to the car to go pick up Mother.

Once home, I headed straight for the shower, while Mother got out of her disguise, shedding the male clothes and using spirit gum to remove her fairly elaborate makeup. We reconvened fifteen minutes later in the dining room at the Duncan Phyfe table, where she put the letter of provenance from the Gabby Hayes photo next to the one from the Earp poster.

We stood, leaning over them, eyes going from one to the other and back again. We were not forensic experts in handwriting comparison, obviously, but we really didn't have to be.

The first part of the photo's letter, written in the 1950s by Judd when he first got the eight-by-ten, was in a strong hand, as was the signature. The added sentence saying Daryl Dugan was now the owner, along with Judd's signature, was similarly strong, written before his handwriting had gotten shaky.

The first part of the poster's letter, written by Judd when he got it just before his death, was with a shaky hand. Yet the added sentence saying Daryl Dugan was now the owner, and signed by Judd, was strong.

But it, too, should have been shaky.

Mother arrived at the same conclusion as me. She said, "Daryl traced the ownership sentence from the photo's letter of provenance onto the poster's letter."

I placed one letter on top of the other and held them both up to the ceiling light.

"Yup," I said. "That's exactly what he did." I returned the papers to the table. "We need to take this to Rudder, or Tony."

Mother frowned. She didn't like relinquishing the reins of any investigation, let alone one so close to its conclusion. But she didn't disagree, at least not out loud.

"Anyway," I said, "I better call Della."

I did, sharing with Pickett's daughter the conclusion we'd reached, but adding that the documents would have to be examined by a police handwriting expert, who could substantiate our theory in court.

"But that'll take time," she pointed out.

"Yes, but it's not like Dugan's going anywhere. And he doesn't know what we put over on him tonight. Do you have a better idea?"

Nothing.

"Hello?" I said to the phone. ". . . Della?"

We'd been cut off. I redialed her number, but it went to voice mail.

Turning to Mother, I said, "I don't have a good feeling about this. Daryl lives down the street from Della, you know."

"Why does that concern you, dear?"

"Think about it. I essentially just told her Dugan was responsible for her father's death."

Mother frowned. "Surely you're not implying she might . . . take matters into her own hands?"

"I have no idea. I don't know her that well. But I do know she loved her father. What if she's going over to Dugan's house, to confront Daryl? Or what if he suspects her of working against him? That could be why I got cut off from Della."

We stared at each other.

Then Mother said, "If she confronts him, or he her, the worst that could happen is that he'd become aware he was hoodwinked tonight. We still have the proof in hand that he's our killer."

"But Della could be in real danger. Like you say, he's a killer."

No-nonsense now, Mother said, "She could be in danger indeed. Let's go, dear."

We left Sushi behind, curled up on the carpet, still in her bandana, a tired little cowhand.

The night was dark with no moon, and I was driving too fast, so fast that I nearly missed the entrance to Stoneybrook.

Della's house was the second one on the right, and I slowed down.

"No car in the drive," Mother said.

"Could be in the closed garage," I replied, and continued on.

The development had no streetlamps, only the lights from other houses to help me find the way to Dugan's home, where I was relieved to see no other vehicles except Daryl's truck and wife Candy's car—both parked in the drive.

I pulled over to the curb and powered down my window.

Lights were on in the living room, and an upstairs bedroom, but all seemed perfectly normal.

"Maybe we overreacted," I said.

"So it would appear," Mother allowed.

I was about to pull away when two muffled shots came from inside the house. The front door swung open, and Daryl staggered out, hands holding his chest, blood spreading across his T-shirt like an awful blossom.

I watched, stunned, as the deputy stumbled down the steps, lurched a few feet, then fell face down on the grass.

While I remained frozen behind the wheel, Mother was already on her cell, giving the 911 dispatcher information.

Then, ignoring my protests to stay in the car, she got out and strode over toward the fallen man. Like any good sidekick, I followed her.

She got down on her knees beside the deputy, took one of his hands, and felt for a pulse.

"He's still alive," she said, adding, "but probably not for long."

Barely hearing her, I was looking at Candy, who was silhouetted in the doorway, a hand behind her back.

As I edged toward the house, her figure slowly retreated within, as if the home were swallowing her up.

A few moments passed, while I considered my options. One was just staying here with Mother and the fallen Daryl. But somewhat against my judgment, I went up the stoop steps, then inside. I paused in the entryway, greeted by deafening silence. Then slowly, hesitantly, I made my way up the half flight to the living room.

In the middle of the room stood Candy, as usual in tight jeans and a low-cut tee, her long, pretty face even longer than usual. The blond woman stood staring at the coffee table in front of her, where a cell phone rested. Her feet were bare, toenails painted a bright blood red. Her right arm hung loose at her side, but the revolver in her hand was held tight—the Smith and Wesson Model 3.

I stood frozen, wondering if I should back down the stairs—she looked dazed but dangerous.

I said, "Candy—are you all right?"

She blinked, looking at me, clearly noticing my presence for the first time. Then she suddenly seemed to notice the gun, as well, lifting it, the barrel angled my way. Chilled, I took a small, tentative step back, and then she dropped the gun, as if it were molten, and it thudded to the carpet.

Rather numbly she sat on the sofa. As I went to sit next to her, I toe-nudged the weapon under the sofa.

"What happened?" I asked her. "There's . . . no one else here, is there?"

"No. Just me."

"So . . . did *you* do this, Candy?"

Her nod and shrug were oddly unconcerned, but her blue eyes were damp. "Daryl was going to divorce me, Brandy," she said.

"He told you that?"

Her eyes went to the cell phone on the coffee table; her expression was accusatory. "No, *she* did. Said they'd been having an affair, and that after he became sheriff they were going to get married."

I leaned forward, picked up the cell, checked the ID on the last incoming call, then replaced it.

Candy was saying, "Not fair. Not right. Not after what I'd done for him."

"What . . . what did you do for him?"

"Well, I got rid of Harriet," she said, "didn't I?"

"*You* tampered with the oxygen tank?"

Candy nodded. "I waited till the nurse with the pill cart had gone, then I came in through the patio. Harriet was napping in the chair, and I removed the washer on the valve seal. But I almost got caught when the manager came knocking, and barely made it out of there."

"Did Daryl ask you to do that?"

She shrugged again. "Well, he had to be somewhere else that morning, didn't he? So no one would think he was involved."

"Why did Harriet pose a threat?"

"She was going to tell Sheriff Rudder how Daryl got the poster."

"How did *she* know how he got it?"

"She overheard Blake telling Wanda. She was a real busybody out at that Sunny Meadow place, you know."

Sirens could be heard in the distance, whines growing to screams.

Candy's eyes turned frightened. "Brandy, what should I do? This all got so . . . so out of hand."

Yeah. Didn't it though. Yet somehow I felt just a little sorry for this awful woman.

"Get a good criminal lawyer," I advised.

I don't know why I felt any pity for her. She killed Harriet, and could have killed me. But there was something sad, even pathetic, about how she'd set her sights on her idea of the good life, climbing one pitiful rung up the status ladder at a time, falling off before she'd achieved it.

Two uniformed officers with whom I was well-acquainted—Scott Munson, tall and bony with a squashed oval face, and Mia Cordona, a black-haired beauty who'd once been my close friend—came up into the living room, sidearms drawn.

I stood, and told them, "The gun's under the couch. The murder weapon. Careful with it. It's old, and a valuable antique."

Mia frowned. "What kind of antique?"

"A loaded one. I'll be outside."

And left.

In the flashing lights of the emergency vehicles, paramedics were placing Daryl's sheet-covered body on a gurney. Mother had been correct—he hadn't lived long after being shot.

A small crowd of neighbors had gathered in the street, moths drawn to the light.

Among them was Della.

I walked over to her.

The faintest bitter smile edged her lips. "Looks like he got what was coming to him," she said.

"With your help, he did."

Her laugh was a nasty snort. "How did I help?"

"By calling that woman and pretending to be her husband's lover."

"Who says I did?"

"She does. And I recognized your number on her cell."

Della raised her chin defiantly. "I'm not sorry I did it."

"I don't suppose you are," I said, "right now."

But she might be, later—her rash act of revenge could very well come back to haunt her.

I walked away to find Mother. For a change the sidekick had a story to tell.

A Trash 'n' Treasures Tip

Expect large crowds at popular white elephant sales, so bring along patience, a sense of humor, and tenacity. Mother also brings a hat pin to move the crowd along.

Chapter Twelve

Destiny Rides Again

A few days later, Sheriff Rudder and Chief Cassato came to our house at Candidate-for-Sheriff Borne's request for an early morning get-together. Snagging both men before either of their workdays began was quite a feat, but Mother managed to lure them with an offer of homemade chocolate babka, from the recipe from Mrs. Goldstein.

Mother sat at the head of the table, Rudder and Tony on the left, me on the right across from them. Sushi was positioned beneath the table waiting for any crumbs that might drop. Mother, of course, was looking for whatever factual tidbits she could shake loose from her guests.

After the babka had been served and the coffee poured, Mother said, "Thank you, gentlemen, for taking time away from your busy schedules to clear up a few things."

As a huge fan of the *Perry Mason* television show, Mother said her favorite part of each episode came in the closing few minutes, with what she called the "loose ends" gathering. Perry and Della and Paul Drake would come together in the office or some favorite restaurant, post-trial, and either Paul or Della would say, "There's still one thing I don't understand. . . ."

Mother, of course, had more than just one question, and directed the first to the sheriff.

"Has the investigation into pharmaceutical abuse at Sunny Meadow been completed?" she asked.

Rudder returned his fork to the plate where a large chunk of babka was already half-eaten. "It has. Blake Ferrell, Wanda Mercer, and Joan Lindle were all involved in selling controlled drugs, mostly painkillers. Joan cooked the books, Wanda either substituted the pills or stole them, and Blake sold the contraband through former jailhouse contacts."

Just as Mother had speculated.

She asked, "I assume Miss Lindle is under lock and key?"

Tony nodded. "And so far has been cooperative."

"Perhaps she'll make a good prisoner," Mother said cheerfully, "when she's transferred to one of our state penitentiaries. I'm sure the prison hospital is always in need of trained staff."

"Assuming," I said, "the controlled substances are also kept under lock and key."

Mother nodded at that, then smiled in a babka-wouldn't-melt manner at Tony. "Anything else you'd care to share?"

Tony looked at the sheriff. "Pete?"

Rudder swallowed a bite of babka, touched a napkin to his lips, and said, "The Lindle woman did clear up a few things regarding Ferrell and Mercer. For instance, Wanda broke up with Blake . . . told him she wanted out of the drug dealing, that she was tired of doing his bidding. She was particularly upset about that wheelchair accident you had, Vivian, knowing she'd been manipulated into playing an unwitting role in it."

"What about George Burnett?" I asked. "Was he involved in pilfering pills?"

"We have no evidence of that," the sheriff responded. "But there'll almost certainly be charges of malfeasance at a later date. The pharmaceutical company he'd been using was supplying Sunny Meadow Manor with counterfeit drugs, some quite dangerous to the patients."

Which could explain Frannie Phillips's remark to Mother about the high number of deaths at Sunny Meadow.

Tony said, "And Burnett admitted to knowing Ferrell had a record, but employed him on the recommendation of . . . you may have guessed this . . . Deputy Dugan."

I asked, "Is there evidence that Daryl killed Blake?"

The sheriff looked sideways at the chief. "Tony? Your area, your call."

The chief mulled that for a moment. "We confiscated the deputy's stun gun, which records a time stamp when used. And that's all I'm going to say in that regard."

"Interesting," Mother said, eyes glittering behind the large lenses. "Of course, the stolen items found in Blake's apartment link him to the murder of Judd."

Tony nodded. "Our working theory is that Dugan hired Ferrell to steal the Wyatt Earp poster, and any money or other valuables Blake found, the thief could keep for himself. But Judd interrupted the robbery and lost his life for it."

The sheriff said, "Neither Ferrell nor Dugan started out with murder in mind. But then things started spiraling out of control."

"The drink receipt you girls found, for example," Tony said, "implicates Ferrell for Wanda's murder."

Rudder said, "We also have a witness who saw Blake at the nursing home late the night of the Mercer woman's death."

"Oh?" Mother asked. "Who?"

A tiny smiled tugged at a corner of the sheriff's mouth. "One Arthur Fillmore. Seems he was returning to his apartment around midnight after a rendezvous with a certain lady on the second floor."

Rarely have I seen Mother blush. She did so now.

"That should be *failed* rendezvous," she sniffed.

Rudder muttered under his breath, "Not the impression he gave me."

Mother's pink cheeks turned scarlet. "I would hope the name of the individual the reprobate is so casually defaming will be left out of your official report, and will go unmentioned in the press."

Rudder, his amusement barely concealed, looked at Tony. "Chief?"

Tony cleared his throat. "I believe we have enough on Blake Ferrell without going down that path."

The men were having some rare fun at Mother's expense. They should have been ashamed of themselves (or not).

I turned the conversation to the subject of Daryl's wife. "What about Candy? Does she face two murder trials— one for Harriet and the other for her husband?"

Neither man seemed to want to take my question. Then Tony said, "There won't be any trial. Not a jury one."

"*What?*" Mother exclaimed.

"Why?" I asked.

The chief raised a calming palm. "What I'm about to share can go no farther than his room, for the time being— agreed?"

We nodded, but Mother was frowning.

"Mrs. Dugan," Tony said, "has agreed to a plea bargain for the killing of her husband. She'll enter a guilty plea for a reduced sentence."

Mother asked stiffly, "*How* reduced?"

"Manslaughter. Five years. No parole."

"Certainly it should be at least *second degree* murder!"

Tony was shaking his head. "Vivian, that's a mandatory fifty-year sentence. She'd have gone to trial to avoid that, and a sharp criminal lawyer could argue involuntary manslaughter, which is only two years. Or even self-defense, or an outright accident."

I could envision the scenarios: Daryl had been threatening Candy with the gun, because she'd learned of his crimes, and they struggled; or Daryl had been showing Candy the Earp gun when it accidentally went off.

I said, "Never mind her shooting that louse Daryl—she murdered *Harriet*! What about—"

Rudder raised the calming hand again. "As for now," he said, "there's not enough evidence for a charge to stick."

"But she *admitted* it to me—how she jimmied that oxygen tank."

Tony said, "Brandy, Candy telling you how she tampered with the oxygen tank isn't enough. It's your word against hers—you know that—but rest assured, we won't stop trying to connect her to that death. That's *not* part of the plea bargain."

Rudder was nodding. "The security cameras at Sunny Meadow, as we know, are nonfunctional. But through traffic and security cams around town, Candy may have been caught driving toward Sunny Meadow that morning. Even an eye witness or two, who might recall having seen her, may yet come forward. But keep that under your hat."

Tony's cell rang, and he stood and left the room.

After a moment the chief came back. "I have to go. Thank you, Vivian, for the coffee and cake."

"Babka," Mother corrected.

"You're welcome," Tony said, and went out again.

I left the table and followed him to the front door, where we stood facing each other.

He seemed a little distant.

"Anything wrong?" I asked. Meaning with us, not the call—unlike Mother, I didn't feel the need to keep up with police business.

A strand of my hair had fallen across one eye, and he gently stroked it back. "No. How about dinner tonight at my cabin? I've got some nice filets."

"What time?"

"Seven."

He twitched a smile and slipped out.

If something *was* wrong, I guessed I'd find out later; in the meantime, I pushed any thoughts of discord from my mind.

I returned to the dining room, where Rudder was on his feet, in the process of leaving, as well.

Mother, still seated, looked up at him. "Tell me, Sheriff, had you suspected your deputy in any of these no-good-nik shenanigans? Was that the reason you'd been so forthcoming with me where earlier information was concerned?"

Rudder didn't answer for a moment. Then, deadpan, he added, "Let me just say, regarding the election . . . you had my vote from the start."

For once, Mother was at a loss for words. Me too. They had been adversaries for so long.

He shrugged. "But of course now, the point is moot."

"Pardon?" she asked.

"You won't be needing my vote to win."

"What do you mean?" I asked.

He glanced from Mother to me, then back to her again. "You don't know? I would think you'd be gloating."

"Know *what*?" she demanded. "And gloating is certainly *not* my style!"

The sheriff and I traded raised-eyebrow expressions.

Then he said, "With Daryl off the slate, Vivian—and it being too late for anyone else to file papers for the position—

you are the presumptive sheriff." He shrugged, adding, "That is, if you receive at least one vote."

Mother gave a loud *whoop*!

"Does Tony know that?" I asked Rudder.

"Yes. I just explained that to him this morning. He's not on top of the county procedures."

Which might explain the troubling vibes I had gotten from him.

Now the possibility of a stress-free, romantic dinner at the cabin tonight had been called into doubt. Seemed that Mother could crash a party without even attending.

Tony and I made it through the meal without a mention of Mother being a bunion-free shoe-in for sheriff, although it permeated the air like the chill evening air breezing in the open window.

Now we were seated on the couch in front of the crackling fireplace, my head on his shoulder, his arm around me, as we watched the flames dance, smoke and sparks drifting lazily up the chimney.

Sushi—whom I wouldn't have dared leave at home, with Tony's name in the air, as it would risk her retribution— was curled up at the hearth with Tony's dog, Rocky, the love of her life, the mixed-breed mutt with a black circle around one eye right out of *The Little Rascals*.

I lifted my head and said, "Let's get married now."

Tony took a long moment to respond. "I don't think that would be such a good idea, Brandy."

Was he punishing me for Mother's indiscretions?

I pulled back a little. "Are you saying that you want to take a breather? Or . . . break *up?*"

"Why . . . do you?"

Willing my tears back, I said, "No to either."

He smiled. "Me too."

I breathed an inner sigh of relief.

Tony went on, "But I'm okay with waiting a while . . . to see how things go with Vivian and this new . . . role of hers."

"You're okay with that?"

"Okay with that. After all, you waited for me while I was in WITSEC, not knowing if we had a future together."

True. So he did sort of owe me one.

I asked, "Want to make a bet with me on what happens with Mother?"

"What are the stakes?"

"Winner gets to choose where we go on our honeymoon."

"Deal," he said.

"I bet she gets impeached or recalled or however it's done around here."

Tony stroked his chin. "I bet she resigns. She'll miss the freedom of going where she wants to when she wants to. She has no idea of the workload she's taking on."

I asked, "Shall we seal the deal with a kiss?"

"By all means."

We did. At least.

The following Saturday, Mother and I held the white elephant sale at the food bank, which was a tremendous success, and all the proceeds were donated to the facility's charity, since Mother now didn't need the funds for her campaign.

Afterward, while Mother was settling up accounts with the food bank manager in the office, I finished packing up the few items that hadn't sold.

A knock came and there was Della, poised in the open doorway. She was in a pale blue pantsuit with a scarf and some beads—she'd have looked nice, in a professional way, if her expression hadn't been so grave.

"Sorry I couldn't make the sale," she said, as she approached. "I had to work at the gallery. But I was hoping you'd still be here."

"Oh?"

"I . . . went to the police station and told Chief Cassato that I'd made that call to Candy, pretending to be her husband's . . . girlfriend. Or lover. Whatever."

I was glad she'd come clean.

"I knew the Dugans a little," she went on, still in the doorway. "Candy, Daryl, and I were on the Stoneybrook owners' association board. So I guess my claim was credible to her, though there was really nothing to it."

Just enough to get Dugan killed.

Della continued, "The chief said there wouldn't be a jury trial because of a plea bargain."

"That's right."

She looked relieved. "I guess that means I won't have to testify about what I did."

Testimony that surely would have worked in Candy's favor, proving the shooting was heat-of-the-moment and dispelling premeditation.

"I want to thank you for what you've done for me," Della said. "Solving Dad's murder, and giving me closure."

"You're welcome," I said. "What will you do with the Wyatt Earp gun, after you get it back?"

Her smile was melancholy. "Send it to the museum along with the knife and pipe. I can't ever look at them again, or make money off them—I have that much of a conscience, anyway."

"Candy's was a crime of passion," I said, "and your reaction to hearing the deputy killed your father? That was an act of passion, too. A rash act. I understand that."

"I wasn't trying to sow murder, Brandy. Just distrust between them so that maybe Candy would expose what he did to the authorities. It just got . . ."

"Out of hand," I said. "All because a collector wanted a valuable gun. And he got it, didn't he?"

She nodded glumly and left.

Mother came out of the manager's office, her gait nearly normal.

"Dear, I feel like celebrating," she said cheerfully. "Would you take me to the Dairy Queen for a butterscotch Dilly Bar?"

I hefted the box of leftover white elephant items. "No problem."

She grinned. "Awesome."

Heading out to the car, I said, "So. All you need is one vote, huh?"

"One vote, dear, yes."

"Well, you know you can count on mine."

She patted my shoulder. "That's sweet, dear. But I'm not worried about whether or not I get your vote."

"No?"

"No. Who do you think *I'm* going to vote for?"

To be continued . . .

A *Trash 'n' Treasures* Tip

Look items over carefully before buying as white elephant sales usually have a "no return or exchange" policy. Mother carries a magnifying glass and checks every inch of her treasures—like any good detective.

Mrs. Goldstein's Chocolate Babka

Dough:

½ cup warm water
2¼ tsp. dry yeast
1 tsp. sugar
5 cups flour
¼ cup packed brown sugar
¼ cup sugar
1¼ cup butter or margarine, softened
2 eggs
1 egg white
3 tbsp. vanilla extract
1 tsp. grated lemon zest

In a large mixing bowl, put the warm water, yeast, and the 1 tsp. of sugar, and whisk together. Let sit for 10 minutes until frothy. Add the remaining ingredients and mix thoroughly. Cover the bowl with plastic wrap, and set dough aside to rise, about 2 hours.

Wet Filling:

1 cup cocoa powder
¾ cup canola or vegetable oil
½ cup boiling water
2¼ cups confectionary sugar

Put all ingredients into a bowl, mix until smooth, and set aside.

Dry Filling:

¾ cup sugar
¾ cup brown sugar
½ cup cocoa powder
¾ cup confectionary sugar
¼ cup flour
¼ tsp. kosher salt
½ bittersweet or semisweet chocolate bar (size 3.5 oz.),
    finely chopped
½ milk chocolate bar (size 3.5 oz.), finely chopped

In another bowl, mix ingredients together until evenly distributed.

Crumb Topping:

¼ cup butter or margarine, cut into small pieces
¼ cup sugar
¼ cup flour

In another bowl, mix all together to make coarse crumbs.

To Assemble:

Divide the dough into 4 equal-sized balls. Roll 1 ball out into a 12-by-10-inch rectangle. Spread ¼ of the wet filling over the dough, then sprinkle ¼ of the dry filling over the wet filling. Roll the dough into a tube, starting with the longer side of the rectangle. Set aside. Repeat for the other 3 balls. Take 2 rolls and make a slit the length of the tube to expose filling, then twist the 2 rolls around each other to make a braid, tucking ends underneath. Place into buttered 12-inch loaf pan, and sprinkle with half of the crumb topping. Cut and braid the other two rolls, put into a separate buttered 12-inch loaf pan, and sprinkle on top the remaining crumb mixture. Bake at 375 degrees for 45 minutes. Cool before slicing. Makes: 2 babka cakes; each serves 8–10 people.

(*Disclaimer:* Neither Mother nor I would ever attempt to make such a time-consuming recipe—Goldie baked the babka for us, as a favor, and for a donation to the Anti-Defamation League. All comments or questions concerning this recipe should be directed to Mrs. Goldie Goldstein at Sunny Meadow Manor—now under new management.)

About the Authors

Barbara Allan is a joint pseudonym of husband-and-wife mystery writers Barbara and Max Allan Collins.

Barbara Collins is a highly respected short story writer in the mystery field, with appearances in over a dozen top anthologies, including *Murder Most Delicious, Women on the Edge, Deadly Housewives,* and the best-selling *Cat Crimes* series. She was the coeditor of (and a contributor to) the best-selling anthology *Lethal Ladies,* and her stories were selected for inclusion in the first three volumes of *The Year's 25 Finest Crime and Mystery Stories.*

Two acclaimed hardcover collections of her work have been published: *Too Many Tomcats* and (with her husband) *Murder—His and Hers.* The Collinses' first novel together, the baby boomer thriller *Regeneration,* was a paperback best-seller; their second collaborative novel, *Bombshell*—in which Marilyn Monroe saves the world from World War III—was published in hardcover to excellent reviews. Both are back in print under the "Barbara Allan" byline.

Barbara also has been the production manager and/or line producer on several independent film projects.

Max Allan Collins in 2017 was named a Mystery Writers of America Grand Master. He has earned an unprecedented twenty-three Private Eye Writers of America "Shamus" nominations for his Nathan Heller historical thrillers, winning for *True Detective* (1983) and *Stolen Away* (1991).

His other credits include film criticism, short fiction, songwriting, trading-card sets, and movie/TV tie-in novels, including the *New York Times* best-sellers *Saving Private Ryan* and the Scribe Award–winning *American Gangster.* His graphic novel *Road to Perdition,* considered a classic of the form, is the basis of the Academy Award–winning film. Max's other comics credits include the "Dick Tracy" syndicated strip; his own "Ms. Tree"; "Batman"; and "CSI: Crime Scene Investigation," based on the hit TV series, for which he also wrote six video games and ten best-selling novels.

An acclaimed, award-winning filmmaker in the Midwest, he wrote and directed the Lifetime movie *Mommy* (1996) and three other features; his produced screenplays include the 1995 HBO World Premiere *The Expert* and *The Last Lullaby* (2008). His 1998 documentary *Mike Hammer's Mickey Spillane* appears on the Criterion Collection release of the acclaimed film noir, *Kiss Me Deadly*. The recent Cinemax TV series *Quarry* is based on his innovative book series.

Max's most current novels include two works begun by his mentor, the late mystery-writing legend Mickey Spillane: *The Will to Kill* (with Mike Hammer) and *The Legend of Caleb York*, the first western credit for both Spillane and Collins.

"Barbara Allan" lives in Muscatine, Iowa, their Serenity-esque hometown. Son Nathan works as a translator of Japanese to English, with credits ranging from video games to novels.